SEE YOU

(A Rylie Wolf FBI Suspense Thriller—Book 3)

Molly Black

Molly Black

Bestselling author Molly Black is author of the MAYA GRAY FBI suspense thriller series, comprising nine books (and counting); of the RYLIE WOLF FBI suspense thriller series, comprising six books (and counting); of the TAYLOR SAGE FBI suspense thriller series, comprising three books (and counting); and of the KATIE WINTER FBI suspense thriller series, comprising six books (and counting).

An avid reader and lifelong fan of the mystery and thriller genres, Molly loves to hear from you, so please feel free to visit www.mollyblackauthor.com to learn more and stay in touch.

BOOKS BY MOLLY BLACK

MAYA GRAY MYSTERY SERIES
GIRL ONE: MURDER (Book #1)
GIRL TWO: TAKEN (Book #2)
GIRL THREE: TRAPPED (Book #3)
GIRL FOUR: LURED (Book #4)
GIRL FIVE: BOUND (Book #5)
GIRL SIX: FORSAKEN (Book #6)
GIRL SEVEN: CRAVED (Book #7)
GIRL EIGHT: HUNTED (Book #8)
GIRL NINE: GONE (Book #9)

RYLIE WOLF FBI SUSPENSE THRILLER
FOUND YOU (Book #1)
CAUGHT YOU (Book #2)
SEE YOU (Book #3)
WANT YOU (Book #4)
TAKE YOU (Book #5)
DARE YOU (Book #6)

TAYLOR SAGE FBI SUSPENSE THRILLER
DON'T LOOK (Book #1)
DON'T BREATHE (Book #2)
DON'T RUN (Book #3)

KATIE WINTER FBI SUSPENSE THRILLER
SAVE ME (Book #1)
REACH ME (Book #2)
HIDE ME (Book #3)
BELIEVE ME (Book #4)
HELP ME (Book #5)
FORGET ME (Book #6)

CHAPTER ONE

Bobette Langdon smiled as she left the gas station in Billings, headed for Bozeman. A sign up above said WINEGLASS – 120 miles.

Wineglass. I sure could do with a glass of red right now.

She'd been traveling all day, on the way from her trailer outside of Sioux City, Iowa, to visit with her twin. It'd been eight months since Bambi had moved out to Bozeman, to work at the Double Q, one of those high-end ranch-slash-spa places for city people who wanted to feel like they were "roughing it" while getting their hot stone massages and bikini waxes in.

They'd had a friend, back in Iowa, who'd been killing it with tips, so Bambi had decided to make the trip. Bambi had always been the brave one, jumping without looking.

Bobette smiled at the thought of Bambi out there, doing hair for those rich clients. She'd called, just three days ago, and gushed about how one client had given her a hundred-dollar tip, for a simple blow-out. A hundred dollars! Bobette barely made that in a week, these days.

The recession had hit their small town hard and now, B&B Hair Designs, the place they'd started together a decade ago, was on its last legs. Bills were piling up. So lately, Bobette had been thinking of following in her older sister's—well, older by two minutes— footsteps.

But she was always the more cautious one. Could she just pick up and leave Iowa, where all her family and friends lived? This, she told herself, was an exploratory trip, just to see. Before this, she'd never been out of the state much at all.

As she drove, she turned some country crooner's song up loud and grooved to the sound of the music. It felt good to be out here, on the open road, with all those possibilities waiting ahead of her.

But Bambi better have that glass of wine waiting for me when I get to the Double Q.

Her eyes started to cross, the yellow line in the center of the road fading in and out, blurring and then doubling. Blinking, it became clearer, only to grow fuzzy again, a moment later.

1

She yawned and glanced at her GPS. She still had two more hours to drive.

Bobette turned on the cold air, pointing the vents at her face. Reaching for the door, she powered down the window and let the cold air slap her cheeks.

That didn't do much, either.

I'm not going to make it.

She sighed and picked up her phone, dialing her sister, so that she could talk to her and keep her awake. Bambi, of course, didn't answer. She'd started dating a bartender at the ranch, a real cowboy, hotter than those guys in that television show. Now, she was a hard woman to get in touch with.

"I did tell her I was coming in tonight," she mumbled against the ring of the phone, then pressed her lips together. Sometimes she felt like Bambi was moving on, forgetting about her.

Bobette let the phone ring through to voicemail and said, "Hey, sis, I'm on my way, remember? But I'm still about two hours out and I'm exhausted. I'm going to find a place to spend the night and then I'll be there first thing tomorrow. Better to be safe than sorry!"

She ended the call, wishing she could taste the tart grapes of the wine she so desperately wanted on her tongue. Instead, there was the bitter taste of that chili she'd had in the diner. Too salty, and it made her burp, but she'd needed something to line her stomach. She should've left on this fifteen-hour drive earlier, but she'd gotten a late start. The hangover was to blame. She'd gone to the local watering hole after a dismal day at the salon and spent all her tips.

Tomorrow. Bambi and I will share a bottle tomorrow.

The next exit was for a place called Laurel Springs. There was a sign advertising a Super Mo-Tel Montana there, right off the plaza, part of a giant travel center, but Bobette wrinkled her nose. As she slowed to the exit lane, she grimaced.

The Super Mo-Tel was not all that super.

In fact, it was downright gross. It looked like it was in the middle of crumbling away—half of it already had, and was nothing more than a concrete slab, blocked off by a chain-link fence.

Lovely. On my first adventure outside of Iowa, I don't want to stay in some crappy old motel where there are fleas and cockroaches and blood all over the sheets.

She'd actually dreamed about it. Bambi had told her that this ranch was totally luxurious, with all kinds of amenities that she could use for

2

free. She'd be able to get a massage, get her nails done, all kinds of things, and it'd be on the house.

Stopping at an old roadside place that smelled like mothballs and cigarettes? Not exactly what she was looking for, but as she pulled off the road and saw nothing but darkness beyond the bright lights of the travel plaza, she didn't think there'd be much of a choice. There wasn't even a McDonald's, and she'd seen one of those at every exit for the past four-hundred miles. Laurel Springs was definitely not a thriving American town.

Then she saw the sign. *Laurel Springs Cozy Cottage Rentals! AAA Approved! Five Star Rating! 2 miles!* with an arrow pointing to the left, under the interstate and into the darkness.

That sounded more like it.

When she got to the end of the ramp, she stopped. The travel plaza was to the right, and there were only a few cars parked there. The only person she saw was a trucker in a sleeveless vest and baseball cap, pumping gas. It looked worse than she'd even anticipated. Like a real hole, even in the darkness. The sign was flickering, and she could see the bright-orange, seventies décor in the lobby.

But it was close, and she was tired as hell.

You know what? It'll be cheap, and easy. I'll just rest my head a few hours and be on my way, and the Super Mo-Tel will be a distant memory.

She navigated into the parking lot and idled there, working up the courage to go in. Of course, there were no other cars in the lot, making her feel like the only one brave or foolish enough to attempt to spend the night there.

"Gross," she muttered aloud. "I'm getting bedbugs in my luggage just looking at that place."

But as she sat there, thinking, she realized she had to pee. From there, she could just see a slightly open door to a bathroom.

Okay. In, and out. And then I'll be on my way.

She rushed inside, sure she'd have to deal with some psycho office manager, but when the bell overhead rang, no one came running. She looked around, sniffing air heavy with the stench of old cigarettes, then rushed to the bathroom. It was gross—and of course, no toilet paper. But she did her business quickly and rushed out, flushing as she went.

"You need a room?" a voice croaked behind her as she went to the door.

"No, no thanks."

3

"I have number six. It's our nicest one!"

She didn't even turn. She rushed outside heaving a breath when she was finally back in her car.

She pulled out. Toward the left, she saw nothing but darkness beyond the interstate. But the Cozy Cottages were there.

Well, I came here for an adventure.

So she headed for them. The street went on for miles, and she didn't see another car, coming or going. Her headlights cut into the night, the mountains off in the distance, but she saw no structures or signs of human life at all.

After about a mile or so, she was sure she'd gone the wrong way. As she was about to turn around, she saw a small gas station, with a single pump, lit by a single light. There was a sign near it, barely illuminated by the light: *LAUREL SPRINGS COZY COTTAGES – CLOSED FOR SEASON.*

She groaned. "Thanks for telling me that," she said aloud, turning back to the interstate.

When she reached the travel plaza, she yawned. She was so exhausted that she'd sleep anywhere, including that disgustingly run-down Super Mo-Tel Montana. But then she saw that the travel plaza sold liquor. Specifically wine. Through the windows, she could see the bottles, lining the wall in the back of the store.

Bobette pulled in there. She was the only person in the convenience store when she went inside and grabbed a bottle of red. *I hate drinking alone. But I'll do it, in a pinch.*

She took the bottle to the cashier, to a man with long sideburns and a completely bald head. He was wearing a sweat-stained t-shirt and a nameplate that said, RANDY. "Hey, Randy," she said with a smile. "I'm passing through. You know of any other places to stay than that Super dive?"

He punched something into the register and smirked at her. "You looking to party?"

"Nah, unfortunately. Just looking to sleep," she said as she handed him the cash and he handed her the bag. "I was supposed to be in Bozeman tonight but can't make it that far. My car has a full tank but I'm running low."

"Ah, gotcha. Well, that place over there might not be anything spectacular, but it's the closest."

"Spectacular? Are you kidding me?"

He chuckled. "All right, it's a dump. But if you're feeling tired . . ."

4

"Yeah. No offense, but it looks like a roach motel. Anything better?"

He shook his head slowly, thinking. "The cottage place closed down a couple years ago."

"So I noticed. Sign's still up, though."

He held up a finger. "There's a pretty nice hotel, next exit up the interstate, if you're heading west. The Montana Pines. My sister works there."

"Oh, really?" She made a mental note of that. "Thanks. Have a good one."

"Ask for Shirley! She's my sister!" he called as she stepped outside.

As she went out to her car, she checked her phone for a message from Bambi. Nothing. And they were supposed to go horseback riding in the morning. Oh, well. Probably with that hot new cowboy of hers. Once Bobette got to Montana Pines and got cozy with a nice glass of wine, she'd check to see what movies were on. She'd have a nice nap and make it to Bozeman bright and early.

That thought in her head, she looked around as she fumbled to get her keys out of her jeans. This place sure was desolate. Her little corner of Iowa wasn't exactly a booming metropolis, but here, the darkness seemed to stretch on forever. It felt like she was on the edge of the world.

She set the bottle of wine in the passenger seat, next to her overnight bag, and started her car. Taking her time to set her GPS, she got ready to head back on the ramp to I-86 West. The highway passed right through her backyard, practically. People called it the highway thru hell. Ever since it'd been built, there were always stories about the road. From gruesome to downright spooky. But she never got into that.

As she set her GPS, an ad came up for The Montana Pines Chalet. It was pretty, at least, from the ad, and they had a free continental breakfast. She smiled. *Now that sounds nice,* she thought. *Not one of those cheesy old roach motels.*

She reached for the key in the ignition.

Without warning, something slipped around her throat, and suddenly, she was gagging.

In shock, she raised both hands to her throat, which spun the steering wheel, hard, to the right. Her hands flailed, waving, almost independent of her body. Tears were squeezed from her eyes, and through her haze of vision she concentrated on the convenience store.

5

Where was Randy? Surely, he could see this, and would come out to help?

But there was display of snack cakes, snow shovels, and propane tanks in the way. She couldn't see the register at all.

The horn. She reached for it, but suddenly, whoever was behind her pulled her, violently, back against the headrest.

She couldn't breathe. She couldn't believe . . . someone was in the car with her, in the back seat, choking her.

Who? Why? The questions built up in her mind; her windpipe was being crushed. The pressure was like a thousand explosions in her lungs. She couldn't even gasp, much less speak, as terror seized her. *This is it. I'm going to die.*

The last thought that occurred to her was that it would've been far safer had she driven all the way to Bozeman that night.

CHAPTER TWO

Something's coming . . .

Rylie Wolf, age nine, felt the back of her neck prickling with sensation. It was a feeling she'd never experienced before, one that made her heart shudder in her chest.

She peered out the window. Sure enough, clouds were gathering in the wide Wyoming sky.

A storm. A storm was coming. She tried to massage the goosebumps away, but they only seemed to pop out more.

No, Rylie, worse than that.

She sat in the massive RV belonging to her neighbor, on one of the bunks beside the kitchen, watching Rose cook breakfast. The abundant sunshine framed her face, lighting up the flowered wallpaper and making everything bright and happy.

"You hungry, Ry?" Rose said, smiling up at her as she scraped scrambled eggs onto a plate. "Sleepy girl. You and Maren and Kiki must've stayed up way past your bedtime!"

Rylie laughed, rubbing her eyes, and looked around. "Where are they?"

Maren was her older sister; Kiki was Rose's daughter. They'd been neighbors, and fast friends—almost like family. Rylie and Kiki had done everything together, so that was why Rose had invited her and her mom and Maren on a "girls trip" in their family RV that summer, tooling about the campsites around Yellowstone. It had been so fun, on the road, like a dream—driving most of the day, hooking up the campsite at night, drinking Cokes and margaritas while they sat by the fire and shared stories.

And then, in that one moment, everything had changed.

The always smiling, cherubic woman with the yellow curls looked to the window, and dropped the pan to the ground with a clatter. Hot oil spattered everywhere.

Suddenly, the clouds rolled overhead, casting dark shadows over the kitchen. Thunder boomed.

"Rylie," Rose warned, wiping her hands on her apron and heading for the door. "Go to the back bedroom now."

She scampered down from the bunk and froze there. She'd always been told that the back bedroom was off-limits to kids. "But—"

"Do it! Now!" Rose shouted in a voice Rylie had never heard her use before.

More thunder boomed, and the earth shook with bright light, as if lightning had struck nearby. It spurred Rylie into action. Her skinny limbs working, she scrambled to the back of the RV and buried herself under the covers.

That was when she heard the rain, pattering against the metal roof of the RV.

Then, the crackle of thunder. Or was it gunshots?

Voices, then. Male. *"I thought there were three?"* one had said. *"Naw. Just those two."*

And then the door had slammed, and after that, nothing.

Nothing for hours and hours. Or at least, it seemed like that. Rylie had been bathed in sweat by the time she'd pulled herself out from her hiding spot. She'd crept to the dirt-crusted window over the RV's kitchenette sink and stared out at the bodies, lying motionless in a circle. Kiki, Rose, and her mother. They'd all been shot, once, in the head.

But no Maren. Maren was gone.

She was still gone, now, over twenty years later. Without a trace.

"They were dead. They were all dead. Covered in blood. And she was gone."

Rylie Wolf blinked from the awful memory, and looked up at her new partner in the FBI Rapid City field office. Michael Brisbane, movie-star handsome and oddly happy-go-lucky for this line of work, stared at her with his eyes wide. He licked a bit of mustard from his sandwich off his cheek, and even managed to look good, doing that. "You're serious?"

She glared at him. She was used to keeping to herself, especially things regarding her past. A lone wolf, that's what she called herself. His reaction was a big reason why she never spoke of it. This had probably been the biggest thing she'd ever admitted, to anyone, and it had been as hard as ripping her own heart out.

But over the past month, living close to where it had all gone down, it had been weighing on her, more and more. She'd come to trust her partner, so she decided that if anyone could finally help her set the biggest mystery in her past to rest, it was him.

"This isn't actually something you joke about," she snapped.

He pushed the Hardee's hamburger that was his lunch away from him and put his elbows on the desk. "Yeah, yeah, you're right. I'm sorry. Which case file is it?"

She went to the pile of files on her desk and flipped through them. Then she pulled one out, handing it to him.

He opened it, and his eyebrow lifted. He wiped his mouth with a napkin as he read. "I just . . . wow. I actually heard of that case, before I even saw the file."

"You did?"

Of course, he did. It had been national news. She didn't mind that, because a lot of people knew about it. But now, it was tied to her, and that made her stomach turn.

"Everyone knows this case," he confirmed. "I was only a kid at the time it happened, but I remember. There was a big manhunt on after it, for the killer, and the missing girl."

She nodded lamely. "That's right."

This was new territory for her. She didn't do this. She never got close to anyone. Even her partners. *Especially* them, because she hated looking weak.

He looked up. "Your sister?"

"Yep."

"Older or younger?"

For a second, she wished she could put the cat back in the bag. But she needed to push through. "Older. If she was alive today, she'd be thirty-six years old."

His mouth formed the shape of an O. He paged through the file some more. "Funny, I don't see . . . and I definitely don't remember . . . any mention of her having a sister."

"Yeah. Because I was young. But I was there. I hid when it happened so I couldn't tell the police much, but I was the only witness who survived."

He blinked. "Yeah? How old were you?"

"Nine. My sister was twelve when she was taken."

"Jesus. That's something for a little kid to go through. But I guess that explains why you're in this line of business," he said, closing the file. "So what do you want help with?"

"I want to reopen it."

9

He shook his head. "You have new evidence?"

"No. But I've been burying my head in the sand for too long. I moved out to Seattle to get away from the memories. That last case brought us right back to Story Creek. That's where it happened, at an RV park around there. What are the chances?" She swallowed. "And after being on this highway, so close to where the murders occurred, I realized—something brought me back here for a reason. I need to find out what it is."

He shook his head. "But that case has been ice cold for two decades."

"And? Now that I'm here, if I dig around Story Creek some more, I bet you I can come up with more evidence."

"You're willing to do that?" He crossed his arms and leaned back in his chair, his pale blue eyes boring into her. "Sometimes it's better to keep the lid on things, Wolf. You never know what might be ready to jump out and bite you."

"I've kept the lid on this for far too long. Believe me, I've thought about the consequences. I'm ready to let it out, if I can, no matter what it does to me," she said, backing to the door. "I'll do it with or without your help; but with, it'll be easier."

He let out a grunt and pulled his burger toward him. Then he shrugged. "As long as we don't have any other cases to investigate, I'll do what I can . . . but I really don't know if it's wise, Wolf, mixing business and personal that way. I'm sorry that happened to you, I truly am. But . . ."

She waited for him to continue. But he didn't, and the more time that passed, the sillier she felt. What had she expected? For him to jump up and hug her? For him to coddle her and tell her it'll be all right?

Well, *yeah*. Actually, she had. She wasn't a hugger, but she'd expected more than this, *certainly*. Here's a guy who gave all the sympathy in the world to people whose family members were simply missing. Practically her whole family had been murdered, while she, a small child, cowered, mere feet away. And yet *this* was the response she got?

It was disappointing, to say the least.

She sucked in a breath and let it out, then said, awkwardly, "Well, then, think about it, and if anything that relates crosses your desk, could you let me know?"

"Yeah. Sure."

She took the folder and held it up to him, silently saying, *I'm taking this with me.* He nodded, so she said, "See you later, Robin."

They'd been sparring earlier about which one of them was Batman in their relationship, and which one was the sidekick. "Okay, Robin," he responded. Even as he narrowed his eyes at her in a playful way, his expression leaked doubt.

He was probably right. After all, even though looking at the file made her queasy and she could only take its contents in small doses, she'd taken enough small doses to know it by heart. What else could she learn from its contents that she didn't already know?

She turned to leave before she got caught.

Not that it would matter. Special Agent in Charge Kit Brandon, her supervisor, had been pleased with the outcome of the last case, so, unlike her previous leadership in Seattle, she was definitely on their good side. But she wanted it to stay that way. And Kit had told her to take some time off.

The second she stepped out into the hallway, though, she ran straight into the diminutive woman with the short red bob. The woman was almost grandmotherly in appearance, but when she opened her mouth to speak, she spit nails. Level-headed but brusque, she didn't take crap from anyone, and she *especially* didn't like to be played. Rylie had only been working under her for a few weeks, and already, she knew that.

"Wolf. What are you doing here?"

Rylie started to speak, but the woman peered in the office she shared with Brisbane and shook her head.

"You couldn't stay away from your partner's pretty face for a single day? I thought I told you to take time off."

"Yes," she spoke quickly, before Kit could bark anything else. "I just came in to have a quick word with my partner about something. Now, I'm leaving."

Kit wasn't one to take anything at face-value. Her eyes trailed to the folder in Rylie's hands. "Is that all? Bringing some light reading material with you, are we?"

Rylie shrugged. "Yeah, there's actually not much to do here in town, being new and all. I figure I might as well."

Luckily, Kit didn't pry into exactly what the case was. She said, "Enjoy your time off. Be sure to take a little time to take it easy," and turned away.

11

Rylie said her goodbyes and headed out into the parking lot of the newly-formed Rapid City, South Dakota, field office. In her car, she set the thick folder down on the passenger seat and sighed. How could she take it easy when her life, since that day, had been so hard? She didn't know how.

And that's why, she thought as she pulled out of the parking lot, *I'm going to do everything possible to figure out what happened to my big sister.*

CHAPTER THREE

Later that afternoon, after a ten-mile run around the streets of downtown Rapid City, Rylie grabbed her third beer from the fridge and went to the living area of her apartment.

She had some work to do. But first, she had to work up the courage to open the file. Usually, after a couple beers, she had no problem.

The FBI had certainly spared all expense while setting up their new digs in Rapid City. First, they had an office that was a former dog kennel, and still smelled like wet animal fur. Some of the offices were surrounded by chain-link fencing and actually looked more like cages. But the living quarters they set up for the agents? Primo. The place was the size of one of her closets, back in Seattle. It was a dark, one-room-studio with seventies paneling on the wall and chipped, dented furniture that might've been rejects from a college dorm room. It looked out onto the parking lot of an auto parts store. The mattress was the worst thing—it actually had an indentation in the middle of someone twice Rylie's size, so if she wasn't careful, she could slip in it and suffocate.

But despite the living conditions, it was a thousand times better than what she'd had to deal with in Seattle with her old boss. Her friend from the Seattle field office, Cooper Rich, was fond of texting her the horror stories about Bill Matthews's incompetence. She relished every one of them.

As she looked at her phone, and saw no messages, she sighed. Take it easy?

Rylie never had liked taking it easy. Idleness made her itchy. Kit might as well have told her to go get dental work. It would've been *something* to do, at least.

Flopping down on her lumpy bed, she took a deep breath and opened her case file.

The first thing she saw was her sister's pretty face. Beautiful Maren, that's what all of her friends and family said about her. And she was. Maren had been twelve when she was kidnapped, but she'd looked older, so to their surprise, grown men had begun to whistle at her on the street. She'd grown like a weed that summer. At the beginning, they'd been relatively the same height, and people used to think they were twins. They had the same dark hair, the same spray of freckles over their noses.

Then Maren shot up three inches, almost overnight, and began developing curves. She started wearing make-up and painting her nails, too, and didn't like walking in the dirt outside the RV unless she was wearing flip-flops. She hadn't wanted to play stupid games with Rylie and Kiki, either; her mother had just said, "Maren is growing up."

Rylie remembered thinking if that was growing up, wanting nothing to do with fun, she'd rather stay a kid.

But she'd had to grow up, almost overnight, when those men came to the RV park in Story Creek, and killed her mother and kidnapped Maren.

After that, her father had been so distraught that he hadn't cared much about her at all. She'd spent the next decade of her life, counting down the moments until she could escape—first to college, and then to the FBI.

She never thought she'd come back to the northern central part of the United States, on highway 86, the Devil's Highway, the Highway Thru Hell.

She stared at the photograph of her sister. She could remember the exact time it was taken, when they were out riding horses at Hal's ranch, which was the property bordering their place. Maren had always been better at riding horses. She'd been better at just about everything.

Rylie wiped at her eye and realized it was wet with unshed tears.

Stupid, she told herself. *Why cry about that? She's been gone forever. Wherever she is, do you really think she's thinking about you?*

Dead. She was probably dead.

It was the most logical answer. And yet for some reason, even after all these years, there was still that little shred of hope.

It would always exist, and a little voice inside her would always be asking, *What if?* if she didn't attempt to find the answers.

She flipped through the pages and read the paragraph, once again, that she could've recited by heart:

Office received phone call at 10:26 am that shots had been fired at location believed to be Story Creek RV park. Arrived at the park at 10:46 am and found two female adults and one child in front of a lone RV in the park, each shot once in the head. Another child was suspected kidnapped by the perpetrator, but there was no sign of struggle or evidence left behind.

14

She swallowed as she read it, then flipped through the photographs of the dead girl, Kiki, her mother, Rose, and finally, Rylie's mom. They were all shot in the back of the head, execution-style, and were all lying face down in the dirt. There were photos of tire tracks and footprints, but many cars and people had been there in the previous days, so there was no telling which ones had been left by the murderers. They'd interviewed Rylie as the sole witness, but Rylie had been so young, and knew very little—all she remembered of the killers was their voices: *"I thought there were three?"* and *"Naw. Just those two."*

She'd replayed those words over and over again in her head. Now, she felt like if she ever heard their voices again, she'd know them instantly.

As she was finishing her third beer of the afternoon, feeling buzzed and a little sleepy, her cell phone rang. She thought it might be Cooper, ready with the next story of Bill Matthews's latest escapades, but it was Michael Brisbane.

"Robin," she said when she answered.

"You're not going to stop calling me that, are you?" he muttered. "Can't you come up with any new material?"

She glanced at the file, then closed it. "Sorry, I'm not in the mood to be creative."

"I wonder why."

"Yeah. I'm driving myself crazy. I'll be happy when I can finally come back to the office tomorrow."

"Actually, you don't have to wait that long. I think I have just the remedy."

She sat up. "You do? What?"

"Kit just handed me a case. It's a few murders that happened outside of Billings, that may or may not be related."

Rylie gritted her teeth. "Kit? Won't she be pissed that you're calling me?"

"No. She knew you were chomping at the bit to get back into it. So she told me to call you. She wants us to head on over there, tonight, if possible."

"To Billings?" She checked her phone. "That's more toward your neck of the woods, isn't it?"

"I'm Missoula," he said. "Closer, but not exactly my neighborhood."

She did the mental math in her head, "Still. Billings. That's pretty far. We won't get there until late tonight, when everything's closed down."

"You telling me you're not interested?"

She snorted. She already felt her senses waking up. The mellow feeling the beer had given her had melted away, and now, every nerve ending in her body buzzed. "Of course I'm interested."

"Yeah, but I know you were interested in your own case. I thought—"

"You might be right about that. It happened a long time ago. I'm not sure what I'll be able to find, now. The best I can do is keep my eyes and ears open." She sat up and grabbed her overnight duffel from the top of the closet. "This, though? At least we got some fresh evidence to go on."

"This might be pretty hard, too, because there's not much evidence to go on. With the first two murders, the local police tried to solve it but the trail went cold. This last one just happened, but it looks like whoever this killer is, he's pretty clean. In fact, from what Kit told me, that's the only thing really tying the murders together, other than the fact that the victims were all traveling I-86, and the crime scenes are pretty clean. So she thinks whoever is doing this is a pro, and that they're moving pretty fast, which is why she wanted us on the case so bad to begin with."

"All right, fine," she said, packing a few rolls of socks and some underwear into her bag. "I'll get my stuff together and we can meet up in a half hour. You want to drive?"

"Yep. Sounds good."

"All right. Pick me up at my apartment and we'll head out."

"Got it. So . . . Batman . . . did you have a relaxing afternoon at home?"

"What do you think?"

"I think you spent way too long looking at that file, and now you're feeling like shit and probably a little drunk."

Damn, she thought. *No wonder he was part of his field office's BAU. He knows me pretty well.*

"Impressive."

"Yeah, yeah, yeah . . . you know what tipped me off? I figured, since you wanted me to drive. You never do that. You like having all the control."

It was true. Which was why she'd never liked having a partner, and why it felt awkward, having one now, especially one who knew her deepest, darkest secret. "I'll see you in a bit," she said, ending the call.

At least another murder to look into will take my mind off the fact that I'll probably never see or hear from Maren again.

CHAPTER FOUR

At near midnight, Rylie sat in the passenger seat of Michael Brisbane's new pick-up, reading through sparse case files as he drove west through the wilds of Montana.

She glanced at the speedometer as he drove. "The speed limit here is eighty," she reminded him, in case he forgot.

Of course, he hadn't. He'd spent most of his life growing up in Missoula, as the story went. So he should've known the speed limit. And though he'd mentioned something about other agents having demons that led them into law enforcement, Rylie didn't think Michael had a single scar, physical or otherwise. His life seemed too perfect. *He* was too perfect, with a smile that practically *tinged* whenever he flashed those dimples of his. No, he was a regular all-American Howdy Doody, the kind of man who'd just gotten into the business because he wanted to be a good guy and put the bad guys away.

So of course she had to poke fun at him, every chance she got. It eased the awkwardness of the day before, when she'd spilled her guts to him.

Why had she done that? He couldn't help her. He'd reacted just the way any sane person would-- with confusion and doubt. What could he possibly do to fix the situation? Talk about something she wished she could take back.

"I know it is," he said, hooking an arm out the window and smiling at the sky. She caught him doing that a lot, getting amusement out of the smallest things. Last week, he'd found a cap to a beer bottle discarded on the side of the highway, and he'd looked at it like a kid with a priceless treasure. A few hours before, it'd been the sunset. Now, it was the stars. "Geesh, that's a pretty sight. My grandmaw used to say that was a picture. And she's right. If I could paint . . ."

"So not only do you talk like your grandmother; you also drive like her," she said, holding up her phone flashlight and trying to tune him out as she buried her face in the first file. If he wasn't good with a gun and hadn't saved her butt before, she wasn't sure she'd have been able to put up with him. "Just . . . keep up with the speed. Maybe if you do, we can get there in time to--"

"Huh? Girl, nothing's gonna be open, if that's what you're thinking. There isn't a twenty-four hour anything near Missoula. Everything's going to be long closed, I can promise you that."

He went on, but she missed half of what he was saying. That was another thing about Michael. He could talk to a wall, until the wall caved in.

"Well, it's still good if we get this early start. That way, we can take in the crime scene, at least. And be ready to question possible witnesses whenever anything opens up."

"Right . . ."

"Wait." She held up the paper. "What about this 24-Hour Ponderosa Travel Plaza?" she said, waving it in his direction. "It says 24-hours right on it."

He raised an eyebrow. "Damn. Time's changing. They didn't have anything like that when I was growing up."

"Well, it's there now. Guess you don't know your home as well as you thought you did?"

He frowned. "Guess not."

"And it's not far from the place where the last body was found. I think we should go there, first."

"Before the crime scene?"

"No. Crime scene, first."

"Yes, ma'am," he said, saluting. "So what's the deal with the last body? Is that the one from Iowa?"

She scanned the pages. "Yes. Bobette Langdon from Sioux City." She wrinkled her nose. "Bobette. What kind of name is that?"

"I don't know, *Rylie*."

She glared at him. "You say it like my name's weird, or something."

"Just about a weird as Bobette."

"I don't think so." She punched the paper. "Anyway, as I was saying . . . wait, it looks like we're in luck. She wasn't found *near* the Ponderosa Travel Plaza. She was found there. A day ago. Strangled. Behind the wheel of her car in the parking lot. Looks like she was headed out to visit her sister in Bozeman, and she never made it."

"Right at the plaza . . . should have witnesses then, you'd think," he theorized. "Of course, places like that aren't exactly Grand Central Station, especially at night. Sister reported her missing, right?"

"Yeah. Looks like it. Looks like the state police interviewed the only night guy, Randy Summer, at the travel plaza, who remembered seeing her and speaking to her. But he said there wasn't anything unusual. She came in, got a bottle of wine, and left. Said she was going to get a room and spend the night at a place up the road. That was all. No one else saw anything."

"Right, right," Brisbane said, nodding. "And I just scanned the other cases, but from what I saw, the other two victims were men."

She paged through. "That's right. One was found dead a week ago. The other, three days ago. One was stabbed. The other was strangled, but manually. Looks like they were all from different places, traveling different directions, for different reasons. And they were found in different states. So . . . what made Kit think there's some connection?"

He shrugged. "Got me. Guess we'll find out."

*

They arrived in Laurel Springs, Montana, at a little after two in the morning. It was easy to find both the crime scene and the last place she was seen alive—the travel plaza looked like the only place around for miles. There was a run-down motel across the street, the Super Mo-Tel Montana, that looked like one of those places that rented rooms by the hour, considering the shape it was in. No cars were parked out in front of it, and the Vacancy sign was blinking quickly, violently.

"Mark my words, Bris. We are not staying there," she said, pointing at it. "That looks all kinds of shady."

"Looks closed," he remarked. "No one's there."

It did. It looked like it had once been a lot bigger, the individual rooms spread out in a U-shape around a fenced-in pool. But a good third of the place had been knocked down, leaving just an L where the office was. All that was left was the cement slab foundation. But several of the standing rooms had boards over the front window. "But the sign is on. So it's got to be open. Why would they waste the electricity otherwise?"

"Yeah, well." He stopped at the end of the ramp and looked up and down the road. There wasn't a single car visible, anywhere. "You'd have to be pretty hard-up to want to stay there but doesn't look like there's that much of a choice around these parts."

"True." She motioned toward the travel plaza, which was also pretty empty, despite a vast parking lot. "This is where the body was found, then. Pull in there. Hopefully the night guy is the same one who was there the night of the murder. A . . ." She flipped through the file. "Randy Summer."

Michael pulled in facing the convenience store and the two stepped out. It was a cold night, the wind whipping across the flat expanse of land, tossing Rylie's hair and stealing her breath. She hurried into the small convenience store, and a gust blew the door closed behind her.

She let out a breath, winded, and combed her hair back into place as she looked around. There was a middle-aged bald man in frumpy jeans and a red vest, placing hot dogs on the rotating self-service warmer. He looked up at her. "It's a cold one out there, huh?"

Behind her, Michael chuckled, blew into his hands, and rubbed them together. "Sure is."

She moved close enough to read his name tag. Just the person she wanted to see. "Randy Summer?"

He froze with his hand on the tongs. "You guys with the police? About that lady who was murdered?"

Rylie pulled out her credentials and presented them to him. "FBI, actually."

His eyes went wide. "Yeah? Never thought I'd see you guys all the way out here in no-man's land. I mean, you guys probably don't have much reason to come out here. Ain't much happening, if you know what I mean."

"You found the body?"

"I did." He whistled. "Damn, it was the craziest, most gruesome thing I've ever seen. Her face was all pale, her tongue sticking out. Her eyes were closed but her neck was in such a weird position. I knew the second I saw her, she was dead. I'll never forget it."

"It said in the report that you interacted with her prior to her death?"

He set the tongs down and dragged a hand down his grizzled, pudgy face. "Yeah. I sure did. She came in for a bottle of wine. Said she was looking for a place to stay but didn't like the looks of the motel over there. Can't really say I blame her. That place is a little sketchy. So I told her about this place at the next exit. Montana Pines? My sister works there. I said it might be more her speed."

"So she was looking for a hotel room, then?"

He nodded. "Yeah. She said she was looking for a place to sleep. I guess she'd been out driving a while. I thought maybe she'd come in and get gas, but she didn't. Just the wine." He hitched both shoulders.

21

"I remember just about everyone who comes in here and what they buy because I only work nights, and we only get a few odd customers. If I get five in a night, that's a regular traffic jam."

Brisbane was staring at the *People* and *Entertainment Weekly* magazines lining the check-out counter. "So what happened after you checked her out?"

He shrugged. "Not much. She just left."

"Can you show me, exactly, where the car was parked when you found it?"

"Yeah. She parked kind of off to the side, in the last space, farthest from the doors." He headed to the door and pointed.

Rylie went to the display of powdered sugar donuts, and leaned over, peering out the window. From the cash register, yes, many of the spots to the left of the building weren't visible, but they became visible, the closer one got to the door. But there was nothing of interest there, just a parking spot, the center stained with what looked like a vehicle's oil leak.

"You have security cameras up front here?" Brisbane asked.

Randy shook his head. "We did. But they got busted up during an armed robbery a couple years back, and I haven't gotten them fixed."

Of course, that would've made things too easy. But it also made her wonder . . . did the killer know the cameras were all busted, to take such a chance? "Isn't it odd, single woman like that, that she would park in that space, instead of one right in front of the building?"

Randy nodded. "Not sure why she did that, but she did. So I didn't see her car until later."

He motioned to the magazines. "I usually do crosswords or read to pass the time, and a new *Star* came in. So I was looking at that, and never really noticed that she hadn't left. It was only an hour later, when I went to restock the donuts over there, that I noticed the car was still there."

"And then?"

"I noticed she was sitting in there. At first, I thought maybe she'd decided not to rent the room after all. Maybe she didn't have the money. I said to myself, 'Oh, hell, here's another one, getting drunk in the parking lot. Bet she's gonna kill someone when she gets on the road.'" His eyes went to the window, and seemed to glaze over. "But the more I kept looking at her, the more I started wondering. Then I realized her eyes were closed, and I though maybe she'd passed out. It was only when I came out to see if she was okay that I noticed. The

22

tongue . . . the marks on her throat . . . I knew right away she was dead."

"And you didn't see anyone?" Rylie asked, imagining the car out there, in that last space in the lot. The lot wasn't well-lit at all, except right in the front windows, and near the gas pump.

"No, I didn't see no one!" he said, his eyes wide. "Didn't hear nothin' out back, either. Never seen any cars leaving or nothing like that. Feel like whoever did it was like some phantom who came out of nowhere. 'Cause there wasn't no one around here at all when it happened. Place was dead, as usual. Anyone comes around here, I notice."

Rylie walked along the windows, past all the displays, to the door, and looked out. "What about that motel over there? You said it's not closed?"

"Nah, it's open. Barely. Henny runs it. She's a crazy old bat, but she ain't got nothin' much else going on, so she keeps it open." His lips twisted. "If you were askin' me, though, I'd say it should be torn down, and she should sell the place. A lot to run on her own. She's got to be ninety by now."

"What happened to it?" Brisbane said, squinting through the glass. "Looks like part of it isn't there?"

"Yeah. There used to be twice the number of rooms there are now. Henny told me that in its heyday, the place used to sell out, every night. But then people wanted fancy chains, and spas, and free breakfasts. She couldn't keep up. Then a few years back, one of the guests on the end there must've left a cigarette burning, because it started a fire. Some fire. The fire department was just barely able to get it under control, but not before they lost a third of the rooms." He shrugged. "Not that it mattered. Place usually only gets one or two lodgers a night."

"And that night?"

"I don't think they had any. That's what I told the police. I didn't see anyone parked out front, from what I can remember. But Henny could tell you better."

"She works that place all alone?" Rylie asked. "A ninety-year-old woman?"

He nodded. "I think. I don't know. Ain't seen anyone else much around there. I don't know her well—she keeps to herself and she's a little batty. But she's a bit of a live wire, that one. I don't think she's got any help, maybe just some people passing through, helping with odd repairs she can't manage herself. She comes in here, every other

23

day, to get milk for her coffee or a hot dog. She's a good girl. Not the murdering type, if that's what you're thinking."

Rylie smiled. "No, I wouldn't consider her a suspect. But we should still check her out and see if she noticed anything. She manages that place all night and day? Without help?"

"Well, it ain't like they're banging down the door to reserve a room there."

"True. You ready, Bris?"

He nodded. "Thanks, Randy."

"Yep, but one thing you probably should know about old Henny," Randy said with a smirk. "You probably don't want to count on her havin' seen or heard nothin'."

"Why's that?" Brisbane said, grabbing a pack of gum. He set it on the counter, along with a dollar bill.

Randy's lips curled into an even bigger smile. "Because the old lady's blind as a bat. She can't even see her hand if it were right in front of her face. Almost totally deaf, too."

Rylie and her partner exchanged glances, and Michael took the words right out of her mouth. "Well, that's just *great*."

CHAPTER FIVE

It was still night when they drove across the street to the Super Mo-Tel. Rylie had hoped that the place only looked shady from afar, but unfortunately, it only got worse as they drew closer. The "pool" was actually just a pool-shaped outline in front of the place, filled in with concrete and weeds. The porch columns were being held up by crumbling cinderblocks. There was what looked like a giant wasp's nest, in the corner of the porch. Not exactly welcoming.

"Sure you don't want to stay here?" Brisbane quipped as she went for the door. He reached forward and grabbed it first, before she could, and waved her in, chivalrously.

Inside, the cigarette smoke was so bad, Rylie's eyes began to water. Though a little bell jingled overhead, no one came to the front desk. As they waited, she looked around at the cigarette vending machine and yellowing sign that said, *We absolutely, POSITIVELY do not accept checks!* that looked like it might have been there before the Vietnam War. Off to the side, through a rectangular archway, was a sitting area with rust shag carpet, and furniture covered in thick plastic.

Brisbane went to the coffee table and peered in a bronze dish there, next to an ashtray full of cigarette butts. He pulled out a yellow-wrapped butterscotch and started to unwrap it.

"You sure you want to eat that?" she asked him, dubious. "It's probably an antique."

"Ah, these things don't go bad," he said, inspecting the disc before popping it in his mouth.

Suddenly his eyes went wide and he started to gag. He doubled over and spit it out into his palm. Rylie patted his back.

"Jesus. I never knew a candy could taste like death."

"I told you," she said, marching up to the reception desk. Since no one had come, she rang the bell.

Nothing.

There was another door, slightly behind the small reception desk. Rylie went over there and tried it, but it was locked, so she went back to the bell and tried it. "You think she might have died?" Rylie asked.

He deposited the candy in the ashtray. "Are you forgetting? The old lady's deaf." He cupped his hands around his mouth and shouted, at an earsplitting volume, "HENNY!"

There was the sound of shuffling of paper and feet, hitting the ground. It seemed to be coming from behind the door. Then, the sound of water running. "One second!" an old voice croaked. "I'm a'coming!"

Then, unmistakably, came the sound of a toilet flushing. The door sprang open, and a small old lady in a Roy Rogers western shirt and cowboy hat bigger than the top half of her body came shuffling out, a large-print *Reader's Digest* under her arm. She was wearing a lariat necklace around her throat, with a silver emblem of a bucking bronco.

"Hey, there, cowpokes," she said, giving them both a once-over as she moseyed over to the reception desk. "My apologies for the wait. You caught me indisposed! You two lovebirds need a room?"

"No, actually, we're from the FB—"

Michael froze. The smell from whatever the old lady had been doing while indisposed crept out a moment after she did. Rylie pressed her lips together, watching Brisbane trying his best not to react.

She tilted an ear toward him. "Huh, Honey? Gotta speak up. I'm a little hard of hearing."

"The FBI," he all but shouted, showing her his badge.

She squinted at it, but then gave him another once-over. "My eyes ain't what they used to be, but you're a cutie. You say you're from what . . . the F. B . . . what?"

"The FBI!" Rylie shouted even louder.

The woman still looked confused, but Rylie decided to let it go. If they had to wait this long to ask every question they wanted an answer to, they'd never finish the investigation.

"Anyway," she shouted, so loud that her own voice rang in her ears. "We wanted to ask you about the murder that occurred across the street? At the gas station?"

Henny squinted. "Eh?"

Rylie sighed and looked at Michael.

"The gas station? Across the street?" He pointed.

She nodded. "Prices of gas are outrageous these days. Good thing I don't drive no more. I get everything I need or want right across the street at that convenience store. Randy owns it. He sets me up. They have great hot dogs." She patted her belly.

"Do you know anything of a murder that happened there the other night?" Rylie shouted.

"Murder, you say?" She stuck her lower lip out, thinking. "There was a murder round here a decade ago. That was something. The girl was stabbed and I—"

"No, this would've been not this night. The night before?"

Her graying eyebrows tented. "Oh. Is that what all them police cars were out there for?" She shrugged. "Don't know nothing about that. Probably some drifter caught a traveler asking for directions. That always happens."

"It was a woman. She stopped at the convenience store and was murdered right there in the parking lot," Michael said. "You didn't happen to see anything or anyone—"

"Eh?"

Michael sucked in a breath, let it out. Even he looked like he was at the end of his rope. "You didn't see anything weird?" He shouted, miming the words the best he could, which just involved him waving his hands maniacally in front of him. "Odd? Any strange people around?"

She shook her head. "We're all odd people. But come to think of it, I did have someone pull up, two days ago. I didn't see who it was because my eyesight's bad, but I saw the headlights. Thought I was gonna get another paying guest. But they drove off. A lot of people do that. I don't know what it is about this place that scares people off. It's nice. Clean."

"Yeah, I can't imagine," Rylie said, looking at Michael. She motioned to the door. The old lady couldn't see or hear well. Seemed to be a little crazy, too. How could she be a good, reliable witness? Not to mention that there were no security cameras to speak of, here, either.

Luckily, Michael seemed to think it was just as big a waste of time as Rylie did, because he said, "Thanks, ma'am. We appreciate your time."

When they walked outside, Rylie let out a sigh and bundled her coat around her to fend off the fierce wind. The sky was just starting to lighten, so that meant they could continue on with their investigation and talk to other possible witnesses, soon.

"That was . . . interesting," Michael said when they were in the cabin of his truck, checking their messages.

"I think the phrase you were searching for was . . . useless," Rylie muttered, paging through the file. "Where do you think we should go next?"

He pressed a button on his phone and raised it to his ear. "Breakfast? I'm starving."

She glared at him. The man was always thinking about food. But she had to admit, she was a little hungry, too.

She was about to tell him that they could get breakfast when he hung up the phone. "That was Kit. She said the sister, Bambi, is staying at the Montana Pines. She arrived to identify the body last night. We can probably stop over there, if you don't want breakfast."

"Why don't we do both?"

*

An hour later, they were sitting in a booth of the Ponderosa, the Montana Pines Hotel's lobby restaurant, drinking strong, bitter coffee and going over the facts of the case.

"It's just as you were saying," Brisbane said as he finished off his massive stack of blueberry pancakes. "This first victim, Neez Ramirez. His body was found in a rest stop near Wineglass. Grandfather, owned a business, was coming back from a hunting cabin he'd been staying at with his two grown sons. And this other one, Nick Costas, young guy, IT professional, was found right outside of a place called Belfry, on the Montana-Wyoming border. He was a transplant from California. He'd only been living in Montana for a year, but he'd gone off for a weekend trip, alone, and wound up stabbed to death in the back parking lot of a fast-food restaurant."

"Hmm," she said. All this, she knew. What was currently captivating her was his stomach. She'd never seen anyone eat so much. Not only that, but he'd gotten a spot of syrup on one of the pages.

She reached over and pulled the pages apart. "You might want to watch what you're doing. We'll never be able to get these pages apart if you stick them together with syrup."

"Sorry. But what do you think? There's got to be something tying all these cases together?"

She nodded. "The crime scenes being so clean, I think leads us to believe that they're done by the same person, who maybe wants to switch things up so he won't get caught. So in essence, his pattern is *not* having a pattern."

Brisbane nodded slowly. "All right. So how would we find a guy who's consciously trying hard to trip us up so he won't get caught?"

"Well, you know, from working at the BAU. Even if he's trying to fool us, he can only get so far, because the truth is, there's a common thread. Him. Right?" She gazed at him, and he nodded along. "So no matter how hard he tries, eventually he'll be slipping up and doing things the way he wants them done, and might not even realize the commonality among all his victims. We simply have to find that commonality."

He'd polished off that stack, but it clearly wasn't enough for him. He dipped a finger in the bottom of the plate and licked the syrup off it. Michael Brisbane was such a kid when it came to eating food. "Okay, I'm in. How do we do that?"

"If we look at the files enough, we should be able to find some little thing—a time, a place, a single detail that they all share. We just have to look closely."

He nodded and lifted a page, staring hard at it, not realizing that the corner of it was about to be drenched in a spot of syrup he'd left on the table near his elbow.

"And not get syrup on everything!" she warned, snatching it away. She closed the file. "It's probably late enough. We should go up and see if we can talk to Bambi."

He opened his wallet and set down a rumpled twenty, then followed her out the door to the reception area of the Montana Pines. This hotel was a nice one, with a three-story lobby and a stone waterfall in the middle of it. It was decorated in, appropriately, a western theme, with abundant cowboy and Native American artifacts like lassos, taxidermy buffalo heads, and patterned blankets on the walls. They'd already determined that if they needed a place to stay for the night, this would be their home base.

They stepped up to the reception desk and Rylie showed her credentials to the clerk there. "Hi, I believe you have a Bambi Langdon staying with you? Could you please call her and ask her to come down?"

"Yes, of course." The woman reached for her phone, and paused. "There's not any trouble, is there?"

"No ma'am," Brisbane said. "We just have a few questions to ask her."

The woman checked her computer, dialed the number, and spoke for a few moments. Then she hung up. "She said she'll be right down."

29

"Thanks," Rylie said.

The two agents went to the big leather sofa in front of the giant fireplace, to wait. Meanwhile, Rylie couldn't stop cycling various facts about the case through her head. "They all didn't live in Montana, but they were all passing through here, at one point or another," she said to no one in particular.

"Yeah. But if that's the common connection, we're screwed, because then everyone on the road is a potential victim. There has to be more than that."

He did have a point. She closed her eyes, trying to find the common thread, but nothing came to her. When she opened them, a tall, rail thin blonde woman in her mid-forties was standing before them. She was the attractive, well-put-together type with perfect hair and nails that could've been Miss USA, about twenty years ago, but even the make-up couldn't disguise her wrinkles, and her eyes were red-rimmed from crying.

"Bambi?" Rylie asked.

"That's me," she said, reaching into her purse for her cigarettes. She sighed when she pulled out an empty sleeve. "Dammit. Pardon me. I've been smoking like a chimney since I found out."

"You came in to identify your sister's body, yes?"

She sniffled. "Yeah. Saw her last night. I was too distraught to drive back to my place in Bozeman."

"You live in Bozeman?" Michael asked.

"Yeah. I work and live at the Double Q, the ranch and spa up that way. I do hair for the guests. And Bobby was on her way to come visit me. I thought she was coming that night, but then she called and left a message saying she was too tired and going to get a hotel. When I called her back, no one answered. And then the following morning, I heard . . ." She trailed off and scrubbed her hands down her face. "I heard that she . . ."

"I understand," Michael said in a soothing voice, patting her shoulder, his voice earnest. This was the worst part of the job, and he was so good at it. Rylie watched how easily he offered sympathy to this stranger, and thought back to her own admission, the day before. Why had he been so cold to her, when he was clearly so good at being sympathetic? He thrived on it. "You're going to be all right, Bambi. You two were close?"

"We were twins," she said, blinking the tears from her eyes. "We would complete each other's sentences. I could sometimes feel

30

whenever she was feeling bad. And I did have a bad feeling, but I don't know . . . I should've answered when she called."

"So she was just coming up for the weekend to see you. Did she do that often?"

She shook her head. "No. Actually, this was the first time. I think she wanted to see what it was like up here, because I kept telling her it was great and I was making a lot of money. She kept making plans but canceling them because she wasn't sure. I told her she could fly, but she didn't want to. I wanted her to come up. I told her I'd get her a job and we could live on the ranch together. That was how we were, always together. We never fought. We ran a business together, until I moved up here, eight months ago. Cutting hair. But we were always in the red. That's when I decided to check out the spa. But Bobby, she was a little cautious. She didn't just want to pick up and leave."

"She was cautious?" Rylie asked.

"Yeah, which is why I don't get why this would've happened to her. You think she would've been extra careful about strangers. So all I can think is that she must've met someone. Maybe she offered them a ride. She was careful, but she was nice, too. Too nice. She might've tried to help that person. I don't know."

"Well," Michael said, handing her his business card. "We're looking into it and we're going to do everything possible to help find whoever did this to your sister. But if you have any questions or think of anything else, give us a call. All right?"

"Thanks," she said, and she even managed a smile at him. Michael had a way of putting every person they spoke to at immediate ease. He even walked her out to her car and made sure she had everything she needed before she headed back out to Bozeman.

Rylie wished she could say the same for herself. Though initially, she'd hated his laid-back attitude and wished he was more of a bulldog, like she was, gradually she'd come to realize that they complemented one another. She was tough, when they needed someone tough. And he was kind and sympathetic, when they needed that. So she let him have this one.

When Bambi had driven out of the lot and Michael jogged back to the front of the hotel, he said, "So, what are we up to now? The coroner? The sheriff?"

"We already have their reports. What else do we need from them?" She'd been compiling a list of victim family members. She showed it to

31

him. "I think we need to go through this list, one by one, and see if we can find that common thread among the three victims. You ready?"

"As I'll ever be," he said, and held out his fist.

She stared at it.

"Fist-bump," he said with a stupid grin. "Don't leave me hanging."

"What are we, in middle school?" she groaned, but gave him one, anyway. Then she grimaced and pulled her hand back. She sniffed it. It smelled like maple syrup. "Seriously? Get a wet nap. You're all sticky."

He wiped his hand on his slacks. "Sorry. Let me wash my hands, then we'll go find a place to hang and start making those phone calls."

CHAPTER SIX

It was a bright, though cold morning, in southwestern Montana. The man smiled as he watched the hippie woman load her things into the car. Long hair, long legs, and explosion of ruddy freckles all over her face, she looked like she belonged in the late sixties, with her headband, hip-hugging jeans and platform boots. She stood in front of the open trunk, gnawing on a thumbnail, deep in thought, as if she could feel something was wrong.

Then she snapped her fingers and returned a few moments later, holding her purse.

Ah, of course. She couldn't possibly forget that.

Apparently, though, Airlia was very forgetful. He'd learned that much from listening in on their phone conversations.

"Don't worry, Brock!" she'd said, making the phone call from the motel room phone. She'd actually had an attorney boyfriend named Brock, who sounded like a total, obnoxious prick. "I'm sure I left it at the last place I stopped. It was a cute little watering hole in a place called Reed Point. I got a smoothie there."

Her boyfriend had lashed her for her forgetfulness, then instructed her, as if she were a child, to give them a call and confirm it was there. So her next call had been to the Reed Point Watering Hole, where it was determined that yes, she had left her phone there. Arrangements were made to pick it up.

She slammed the trunk, then went to the passenger-side door and tossed the purse in, along with a couple of bags of snacks for the road. Then she wiped her hands together and reached into the pocket of her hip bag for her keys, doing a little shimmy-jig, likely to prepare herself for the many long hours she had ahead of her, in the car.

Unbeknownst to her—unbeknownst to all of them, he was watching.

He'd watched quite a lot, from his hiding place. It was his hobby. His passion.

He'd always loved observing animals in their natural habitat, undisturbed. They always did the most interesting of things. Things that

33

surprised. Things that confounded. Every little detail was important, so he took careful notes.

This specimen was an interesting one. He couldn't say he liked her. Not really at all. She had a horsey laugh and she was far too opinionated, thought too much of herself. But she was amusing, at least.

In a short time, he'd learned so much about her. Her name was Airlia Birnbaum. She was twenty-three and had just graduated with her master's in Philosophy from Berkley. She was on her way back home to the east coast, and her prick boyfriend Brock, who'd already begun working as a civil rights attorney in Boston. The plan was to live together at the place her daddy had left them in the Back Bay until they decided whether to get married. Truthfully, though, Airlia didn't want marriage. Like she told him during last night's phone conversation, she was much too strong and independent—well, with Daddy's money—to be tied to any man.

Despite the fact that she was a complete ditz who'd lose her head if it weren't screwed on.

He'd also learned other things. Smaller things that she might not have known about herself. One, she was reckless. She thought she was being smart, but some of the things she did were really quite naïve. She was completely oblivious to anything that wasn't her own reflection in the mirror, or else she might have seen . . .

She hadn't, though. She'd sat up late last night, chowing down on Doritos and a burrito she got from the convenience store. She'd watched a *My 600 lb. Life* marathon, probably to gloat about the fact that she didn't have any problems in the weight department. She braided and unbraided her long, strawberry blonde hair, and spent a good amount of time practicing for selfies in front of the mirror, since she couldn't actually take them without a phone and post them to her social media account. He could almost see her itching from the withdrawal.

And the whole time, he'd only become more and more convinced that she was the one.

This morning, he woke bright and early, in time to see the blue VW Beetle with the COEXIST bumper sticker, as it pulled away from the gas station, headed onto the highway, back toward Reed Point, to retrieve her phone.

He'd left her a little gift. He hoped she'd like it.

34

Knowing her, she probably wouldn't even know it existed. But that didn't matter. He'd enjoy it.

The last one had been so good. He'd been much more daring, that time, taking the woman in the parking lot of the gas station. She hadn't noticed the gift he'd left her, either. He'd planned to follow her, as far as he could, down the highway, but then he'd gotten an even better idea.

She'd been reckless, too. She'd left the back door of her car open. It had been so easy to slip in, unnoticed.

He liked them, that way. The easy way.

His first kills had not been easy. They hadn't been messy, but he'd never been messy, even as a child. He'd just been too afraid of making a mistake, so he'd planned everything out carefully, waiting to strike until he could barely stand it. But they were getting easier. Practice makes perfect. Selecting the perfect victim was an art. And it was true. The best thing was, because he wasn't reckless, because he was so careful, the police were completely at a loss. He switched things up. Did things differently so they'd never suspect anything. He'd been playing around, right under their noses, all this time.

Now, he couldn't wait for his next kill. He felt certain he could do more, faster, and be absolutely fine. The police would never know.

This time, he'd go back to stabbing, maybe. He liked the feeling of holding a person, hands tight around their neck, until they breathed their last. But he'd also enjoyed the scrape of the knife against bone. The way the body seemed to cave in on itself, skin giving way, erupting like a popped pimple. The blood.

Oh, the blood was his favorite thing. If he could, he would bathe in it. It made a murder seem more like a murder. More gruesome. More ostentatious. More everything.

Maybe he'd just slash pretty Airlia's long, swan-like neck. Put a big, red, bloody gash in her throat.

But keeping his victims for too long would be risky, and his aim was not to get caught. He liked this too much. He wanted to do it a hundred times. A thousand.

And right now, he had his little hippie girl Airlia, heading east, toward that prick boyfriend of hers.

Running to his car, he jumped in and turned up the radio so loud, it hurt his ears. He started his car and pulled out, following her onto the highway. Airlia was probably listening to Bob Dylan or something she

35

thought made her sound deep and interesting, thinking about that big kiss she'd give her guy, when she finally saw him again.

She wouldn't get that far, though, of course.

He'd make sure of that.

CHAPTER SEVEN

Rylie slumped against the passenger-side door of Michael Brisbane's car, sticking a finger in her left ear so her partner wouldn't throw off her train of thought. He was asking the same questions of another family member of one of the victims, and after interviewing several people, she'd lost track of what she had or hadn't asked this one.

"Hello, Sabina? Sabina Lopez?" she asked, balancing the file folder on her knees.

"Yes," a tentative voice said. "Look, I don't want any—"

"This isn't a sales call. This is Rylie Wolf from the FBI. I'm calling to ask you a few questions about your fiancé, Nick Costas. Is now a good time?"

A pause. When she spoke, her voice was toneless. Emotionless. "Yes, I suppose. Have they found anything?"

"I can't say that they have, but that's why they brought us on. So that we can try to find who did this to your fiancé."

"All right." She sounded rather wary. "What do you need to know?"

"You were engaged to be married to Nick. And yet you live in California and he was in Billings. Is that right?"

"Yeah. I'm at UCLA. I was going to come out there and join him when I graduated next May."

"I see," she said, as Michael started to say, *No, no, no, I understand that. Please, calm down,* in her ear.

She looked over at him. He was pounding his thigh in frustration. Then he ended the call and set his phone down. "She didn't speak English. She thought I was ICE, I think."

Michael rarely got frustrated, but he had good reason to. They'd been going down a list, making phone calls to all the victims' family members, for two hours, and had found little information. Most of the people hadn't answered their phones, so they'd left messages. Now that she'd finally gotten in touch with a live human, Rylie hoped their fortunes were turning around.

Who? she mouthed, then spoke into the phone. "Can you tell me when you last spoke to Nick?"

Brisbane mouthed, *sister,* and crossed out the name on the list of relations of the first victim, Neez Ramirez. Apparently, they were very hard to get in touch with. The two grown sons of the grandfather still hadn't called them back, so they'd had to scrape the bottom of the barrel—a sister that lived in Mexico City. It was probably worthless, anyway.

Sabina's voice came through the line. "He called me from the road during his big weekend trip. He worked all the time so when he finally got a day off, he said he was going to go on down to Yellowstone and check it out. It was one of his bucket list items, he said. He never made it, though."

Michael's phone began to ring. He glanced at it and answered, "Brisbane, here. Oh, Hi. Mr. Ramirez . . ."

Good. One of the sons was finally getting back. Maybe now they could put some pieces of this puzzle together. She put a finger in her ear and concentrated on her line of questioning. "Did he tell you what he planned to do?"

"Nothing more than just going down there. He liked to fly by the seat of his pants. He said he'd sleep in the car, if he had to. But I told him that was dangerous and that he should get a place to stay. So he promised he would." She sighed loudly. "So he did."

"He called you from his cell phone?"

"No, he didn't have a cell phone. One of the only people in the world who doesn't, right? When he called, it was from a rest stop. He joked about some terrible food at a greasy spoon diner he'd eaten, and how he was thinking he might have the runs, so it might take him a little longer, if he had to stop at every rest area on the way. And then he said he'd call me when he made it to Yellowstone, but he never did. I assumed he forgot and was so in awe by the scenery. And then I got the call from the police . . ."

She let out a noise that sounded like a sob.

"It's so terrible. I don't know who could've done this. Nick was such a good guy. A helpful guy. I can only think that he stopped to get gas or something, talked to the wrong person, and they pulled a knife on him. That's all."

Rylie opened the map and followed the line of the highway. The town of Belfry, where the body of Nick Costas had been found, veered off from the Laurel Springs exit off I-86, heading for Yellowstone National Park. It made sense that he was headed there.

"He never mentioned any suspicious happenings when you spoke to him? Dangerous drivers, run-ins, odd people he might've met?"

"No. Nothing like that. He kept talking about how he couldn't wait to be in the park and see Old Faithful."

"Do you happen to know where he spent that night, or anything about the gas stations he might've stopped at?"

"No. I don't. He called me from the road, though, so he must've found a public phone somewhere. Can you look into those records? I saw a television show like that, once."

"Thank you," Rylie said, as Michael began to pound his fist on his thigh harder. She guessed it wasn't going so well for him, either. Turning to face the window, she added, "If you can think of anything else, I'll give you my number."

She recited it, thanked Nick Costas's fiancé, and ended the call to find Michael staring out the front windshield, talking deep, calming breaths.

"So . . . that went well?" she asked him.

"No, it didn't. Neez's oldest son, Ed, is a bit of a . . .," he paused, trying to find the right word. "Let's just say he's not all that helpful. Kept going on about how law enforcement has its thumb up its butt. Stuff like that."

"Oh," she said, as his phone began to ring again.

She glanced at the display and compared the number to her phone list.

Then she held it up to him. "Younger brother."

He waved it away. "Kill me now."

She was hoping he'd say that. "I'll take care of it." She answered. "Hello, Rylie Wolf, FBI."

The voice that answered was a lot more pleasant than she'd expected. "Hi, uh . . . I was looking for Michael Brisbane? This is Manuel Ramirez. He called me to ask some questions."

"That's right. I'm his partner. Do you mind if I ask you some things about your father's murder?"

"No. Not at all. I appreciate you trying to help."

He didn't sound so bad at all, compared to his nightmare brother. "Great, thank you. So your father was coming back from his hunting cabin?"

"That's right. He lives in Bozeman, and he has a place on the Canadian border. We usually go up there some weekends, hunt, and then we all go our separate ways. I live only a few miles from the place. He left Sunday afternoon to drive back to Bozeman on his own. Takes about twelve hours to get there and back. I didn't realize he never made it home until his housekeeper called me and said he wasn't answering the door. Then I got the call that they'd found his body."

"So you didn't speak to him after he left, Sunday afternoon?"

"No, I did. He was worried about one of my kids, who had a cold. So he called me on the route. I think he was outside of Billings. It was late by then. Probably after ten. I told him she was asleep and her fever had broken, and it looked like she was going to be fine. He said that was great, and that was the last time I spoke to him."

"So he probably drove that route often, right? Knew it like the back of his hand."

"Yep. We've had that cabin since I was little. Isn't much. My mom never liked it when she was alive because it doesn't have electricity or running water. But us guys liked it. We went up there at least once a month in the summers."

"Okay. So he didn't mention anything odd that he might have witnessed during this last drive?"

"Anything . . . odd? Like what?"

"A creepy person, something out of the ordinary. Anything, really, that wasn't like all the other times before."

"Actually, now that you mention it . . ."

Rylie straightened. Whenever she heard those words, she knew to pay attention. It usually meant she was on to something. "Yes?"

"When he called me, it was from a rest stop outside of Billings. He had to stop and you know, use the facilities. But before he could get to the restroom, there was some crazy guy, he said, at the stop, marching back and forth, shaking his fist in the air and murmuring to himself.. I told him to get in his car and get out of there, so he did. Said he'd stop someplace else. Never got to use the restroom. That was that."

A creepy guy. A strong feeling of déjà vu gripped Rylie. She'd heard that before. Or seen it. But where? "Did he tell you anything about what this creepy guy looked like?"

She started to shuffle through the papers, looking for it. As she did, Michael said, "What? What's going on?"

"No. Just that he was creepy. I didn't think anything of it at the time . . . " He trailed off, clearly deep in thought. "You think there's something in that, Agent?"

"I don't know. But thank you. I'll look into it."

She gave him her number in case he thought of anything else, and ended the call. The second she did, Michael pounced. "What's going on?"

"Here," she said, lifting a page from a cold case file of a girl whose body had been found, a year ago, near Wineglass. "This girl. Bonnie Franklin. She was murdered last year, and before she went missing, she called her father and told him she saw a creepy guy at a rest stop near Billings, who was mumbling to himself and shaking his fist. She was found at a place called Ponderosa Bluffs."

"And . . .?"

"And a crazy guy like that, shaking his fist and mumbling to himself, was exactly who Manuel Ramirez just told me was at the rest stop before his father was murdered."

"Seriously?" He frowned. "Wow. You got more information than I did out of that family. I'm jealous."

She shrugged. "It pays to not be so nice."

He shook his head. "Sorry. It's not in me." Then he smirked. "So, what do we need to do, now?"

She pulled her seatbelt on and motioned to him to start the car. "I think we should try to trace Neez Ramirez's route, from his cabin on the Canadian border, and find out which rest area he stopped at."

"It's a plan," Michael sighed, pulling out of the parking space.

CHAPTER EIGHT

Rylie stared at her GPS as they drove toward Billings, her ringing phone to her ear.

"You really think this guy's just going to be hanging out at whatever rest stop we go to?" Michael was saying. "If he's the killer, he's not just going to be sitting there, waiting for us to come get him."

"Obviously," she murmured. "But the fact remains that he saw Neez Ramirez. So he's our best bet."

There was a click at the other end of the phone, and a voice said, "Hey, Rylie."

"Hi, Beeker. Can you give me an idea of the rest stops around Billings, on I-86?"

A pause. "Nice to talk to you, too, Ry. Cheery as always."

She rolled her eyes. Beeker was the young IT guy on their team. He and Michael had a bond, but she'd yet to establish much of one with him. She just hadn't had the time. "I'm sorry," she said, with only a hint of sarcasm. "How are you, Beeker? Doing well? The FBI isn't working you too hard?"

"Not too hard," he mumbled. She could hear him typing in the background. "And . . . sent. You should see it in your email box in a minute."

"Thanks, Beeker. You have a nice day."

She ended the call and flipped to her email account. Sure enough, the email from Beeker was just arriving. She opened it and scanned the list. Only three within a fifty-mile radius. That wasn't so bad. "Okay, so the closest one is coming up right here. Split Creek. Turn here. Here!"

Michael glared at her as he pulled off on the ramp. "Yeah, I couldn't tell from that giant sign that said Split Creek Rest Area."

He veered to the side of the road. When the trees parted, they found themselves in a barren stretch of space with nothing more than a parking lot and what looked like a bus shelter. There were a couple of rotting picnic tables out in the field, as well as a rusting metal garbage can. That was all.

"Well, it did say 'No restroom facilities' on the sign," Michael said, looking around. "You want to get out and look around?"

She shook her head. Unless the man in question was hiding behind the garbage can, he was not there. It felt like a waste of time. "Let's go on to the next one. It's fifty miles up I-86."

He groaned. "I'm getting hungry again."

"I know," she said. He *always* was. "Maybe they have a vending machine with candy bars at the next one. I have some quarters."

*

The next rest stop, Ponderosa Bluffs, past Billings, was a little livelier.

Rylie pushed up her sun visor and took in the scenery. "This is where that girl, Bonnie Franklin, was found murdered," she said.

"Here?"

"Yep. The case file says her body was found in the woods behind the restrooms. She'd been beaten to death."

Knowing there'd been a dead body found there should've made the place more foreboding. But it was quite a bit nicer than the last rest stop. This one was in the middle of a forest, with trees blocking it from the highway. There were a few cars, parked in the lot. A couple of families, eating their lunches on the picnic benches. A squat, cinderblock building with restrooms, which had an alleyway in between the women's and men's sides with vending machines.

"Well, even so, this is more like it," Michael said, extending his palm to her.

She stared at it. "What?"

"I believe you said you had quarters?" He batted his eyelashes.

"Oh, right." She pulled some out of her purse and handed them to him. "Always thinking with your stomach, Bris."

"Sure, that's the best part of me," he said, patting it under his blazer as he stepped out. Before he slammed the door, he scanned the area. "You see anything?"

She'd been looking from person to person since they pulled up. "Nope. Looks like a bust."

"Well, we still got one more to go," he said, slamming the door and heading for the vending machines.

She sighed, opened the door, and slid out of the truck to stretch her legs. As she walked idly up and down the sidewalk, she wondered if this was a waste of time. A crazy man, who liked to spend his time at rest stops? He was likely homeless. And if so, he probably wouldn't have the resources to perform all these clean killings.

Maybe they needed to go back to square one and try to think of another tack.

She was just about to head to the bank of restrooms and tell Michael that when she saw something move, in the woods behind the building.

It was nothing, barely a flash, and yet it wasn't anything natural. It was a shock of bright orange, among all the dark green of the pines.

Squinting to get a better look, she decided to get closer. There was a steep embankment past the railing astride the sidewalk. She climbed over the rail and carefully made her way down the slope, to level land.

When she was there, she looked up toward the truck. Michael still wasn't there yet. *Probably that life-or-death decision of what candy bar to get,* she thought. Not that it mattered. This was probably nothing. Just a hunter's vest or piece of garbage from someone's picnic, left behind.

But as she drew closer, the orange appeared, and began to move slightly. Not like something blowing in the wind. The movement was more erratic, more human.

"Hello?" she called as she reached the tree line.

She pushed aside a branch and saw a man, pacing back and forth in a violent way. He had on a dark skull cap, which pushed his stick-straight silver hair into his bushy eyebrows. His hands were thrust into the pockets of his orange hunting vest, and his jeans were dirty. He was mumbling something about "Damn highway travelers, always taking up space."

It was him.

As she was standing there, trying to decide what to do, he turned and saw her. His glassy blue eyes narrowed to slivers and he bared his yellow teeth, showing gaps where a few were missing. "Who are you?" he snarled.

"I'm Rylie Wolf, from the FBI," she said. "I'd like to ask you some questions."

He snorted and fumbled around in the pocket of his vest. "The hell you will."

He pulled out a handmade shiv and pointed the blade at her. "Maybe I'll skin you alive, first."

She held up her hands. "I don't want to hurt you. I just want to ask you some questions," she repeated.

"No questions," he spat out, taking a step toward her. "You're gonna die."

Instinctively, Rylie's hand went to her hip, for her pistol. Her hand, gloved in sweat, wrapped around the handle.

"Let's not get crazy," she murmured to the man, though she had a feeling he already was. She spread her stance, getting into fighting position as he began to advance. "Put the weapon down and no one will get hurt. I just want to talk."

The second she said it, the man let out a long, harrowing war-cry and started to charge.

In shock, Rylie fumbled for her gun. The man reached for her and brought the blade swinging down in front of her face, slicing at her, cutting through air. He let out a horrible, echoing wail, opened his gaping black mouth, and screamed at her with such force that the air it expelled blew her hair back.

She went to shove him back again, in effort to get away. But it felt as though his hands were everywhere, grabbing at her. She felt the blade scratch against the skin of her upper arm, and curled away, frantic. Adrenaline pumping through her veins now, she wheeled on the man and delivered a clumsy but effective kick to his stomach. He sputtered, falling to the ground as if he'd just taken a cannonball to the gut, and dropped his blade.

As she approached, the man hissed so loud it shook her eardrums. Rylie brought her foot down hard, on his back, and leaned over. The man let out the start of a wail, and then stilled as she whispered, "What the hell was that all about? Is that your normal reaction when someone says they just want to talk?"

His hands were fisted above him as he lay there, on his stomach, wailing in rage. His face, half-pressed into the earth, was bright red. "Get off me, you stupid bitch! I'm not telling you nothing!"

She grabbed for her handcuffs, but as she did, she released some of the pressure on his back. He took advantage of it, rearing up, sending her suddenly staggering back against the rough bark of a ponderosa pine. As she grabbed for her gun, he reached the shiv on the ground. and spun toward her, a crazed look in his eyes.

"Don't!" she said, cocking her gun. "Stay right there or I'll shoot!"

His eyes looked through the gun, as if it were invisible. They locked on her. He smiled widely. Then, arms up, like Superman, he lunged.

She nearly squeezed the trigger, but in the last second, a dark blur ran across her line of vision, slamming into the man's side and knocking him to the ground.

She blinked into focus the sight of Michael Brisbane, wrestling the shiv from the man's hand. It wasn't much of a fight. Within seconds, he'd subdued the man with his hands behind his back and taken the weapon from him.

"What the hell do you think you're doing, pal?" Michael said to the guy in his low, Clint Eastwood bad-boy voice. "Attacking an agent like that?"

"Let me go! Let me go!" he screamed, so loudly that people at the rest stop were starting to notice.

She sighed. "Just shut up." As relieved as she was that she hadn't had to pull the trigger, she was still a bit miffed that she hadn't been the one to take him down. She motioned Michael toward the truck. "Let's bring him over to that bench to question him."

Brisbane nodded, snapped a pair of handcuffs on him, and nudged the man over. "Thanks a lot, pal," he muttered as they walked. "You made me drop my Milky Way."

Rylie gave him a look. "Oh, the tragedy."

CHAPTER NINE

Ten minutes later, Rylie stood in the grass, listening to nothing more than the sound of highway traffic passing by, occasionally punctuated by the shrill cries of glee made by kids from a passing family from Vermont, playing tag in the field on the other side of the restrooms.

"Are you going to answer any of our questions?" she prompted, after watching him in silence.

The man sat at the picnic table, shoulders slumped, cuffed hands in front of him, trying to pick the dirt out from under his fingernails. Occasionally, he'd lift his hands to his mouth and tear off a dirty fingernail, then suck on his fingertip. "Nope."

Rylie exchanged a glance with Michael, wishing he'd use his tough Clint-Eastwood voice to get the guy to speak. But he was standing there, just like her, arms folded in front of him, as if they were both waiting for a Whack-a-Mole to pop up.

Finally, her patience ran out. "You'd better tell me if you don't want us to take you in. Or worse."

He chuckled. "Why would you do that? I ain't done nothin' wrong. I tell you, I'm innocent. What's the problem?"

She smiled widely at him and spoke as pleasantly as she could. "I'll tell you what the problem is. You charged at me with a knife. That alone could send you to jail for a long time. And if you're not willing to cooperate with us, we can make things even more unpleasant for you. So, all you need to do is answer a few questions. You can answer them here, or at the police station. But I promise you, it'll be a lot easier for you if you answer them now." She paused to let that sink in, and then continued: "So let's start this again. Your name?"

To her surprise, he shrugged. "Ethan. Ethan Brimley."

"Okay, Ethan, good," she said, as she watched Michael take out his phone. She assumed he was putting in a message to Beeker to see if the guy had any sort of criminal record, which is what she would've done. "Now we're getting somewhere. Where are you from?"

"From everywhere."

"You're homeless?"

"No known abode." He grinned and bared those missing teeth again. "That's what they say in the court documents."

"Court documents?"

Ethan glanced over at Michael. "I'll save you the trouble. I've got a rap sheet that'll make you want to cry. Sure would make my momma want to, anyway." He seemed proud of the fact. "Always looking to add to it, but whatever you're thinking I've done, I haven't done."

That could've been promising, but it was leaving out one major, glaring point—if this man was homeless, he probably didn't have a car. So it wouldn't be easy for him to get from place to place. "How do you get around? You have a car?"

He shook his head. "I don't. I like to stay right here, in my kingdom. People give me money. And I got everything I want right here. Food. Shelter. Toilets." He pointed to the restrooms.

"The police probably don't want you here," she warned.

"Maybe. Thought you were the police. That's why I hide in the woods. Most of 'em leave me alone."

"Do they?"

"Yeah. Most of 'em know this is my domain. I'm the ruler of this kingdom. My queen has yet to be found." He raised an eyebrow at her.

She ignored the comment and glanced at Michael, who looked more amused than disgusted. She couldn't understand why. This man was clearly insane. "You realize this is a public rest stop, right? Owned and maintained by the federal government?"

"That's what they'd like you to think, because the lizard-faced aliens have taken over their brains."

"Ah," Michael nodded. "I've heard about them. But I've never actually seen one."

"Of course, because you're weak-minded, unlike me. I can see through their façade. That's why they don't try to come near me. They know I'm too powerful."

Michael laughed. "Right. Of course." He motioned to a family, enjoying snacks at their mini-van, across the parking lot. "And what about those people? Are they threats to you?"

"No. I'm not threatened by anyone. It's only because I'm a kind and gentle king that I let these traveling people use my resources. Even though they sometimes mess the place up." He wrinkled his nose.

She placed a foot on the seat of the bench across from him and rested her elbow on it, leaning forward. "So, you remember some of the people that stopped here?"

He grinned. "I remember every single one of them! Especially if they don't give me money. Those are the ones I scare out of here. To use my kingdom's amenities, you need to pay taxes!" He laughed, but it ended in a phlegmy cough.

"You remember this guy?" Michael said, showing him a photograph of the murdered man, Neez Ramirez.

He squinted at the photograph. "Yeah. Old guy was a real prick. Wouldn't pay."

"Did you scare him off?" Rylie asked.

"Sure did. Well, tried to, until he got his hunting rifle out and told me to get lost." He shrugged. "So I let him go. Him and his fancy pick-up truck."

That made sense. He'd been found murdered in his pick-up, near Wineglass. "You see him talking to anyone?"

He shook his head.

"You sure you didn't follow him?"

Ethan fixed her with a smooth gaze. "Now why would I do that? You think I'm the kind of king who abandons my kingdom?"

"So you haven't left this place, ever?" Michael asked, raising an eyebrow. "How long have you. . . uh . . . been king of this realm?"

He counted on his fingers. "A year. Just about a year," he said, staring up at the gunmetal gray sky.

Rylie paged through her phone and pulled up a photograph of the other girl, Bonnie Franklin, who'd been murdered a year ago. "What about her?"

He stared at the photograph for only a blink. Then he looked away. "Don't know her."

"If you were here a year ago, you must've seen her. Her body was found—"

"I didn't," he snarled. "I got nothing to do with her."

Brisbane raised an eyebrow and came closer. "You sure about that, buddy? We're supposed to believe you don't know what goes on in your own kingdom? She was murdered here. You must know something."

He looked down at his hands, then put them in his lap. "Don't know nothing."

49

Rylie leaned in. "I think you're lying. I think you know exactly what happened to her. What I don't understand is how the police never saw it."

His eyes shot up to hers. "The police never saw nothing. Because I didn't do nothing."

Michael looked around. "How's that possible? There's only so many places you can be around this rest stop. How's it a girl was murdered and you didn't see that?"

He didn't answer. His body trembled.

"I bet you did see," Rylie continued, liking the way she and Michael were playing off one another. Their back-and-forth tennis match of pressure seemed to be having an effect on Ethan, because he was clenching his jaw and shaking even more violently, now. "I bet you know exactly what happened to that old man Neez—"

"I didn't kill him!" He exploded, jumping to his feet. "I may have gotten the girl, but that was an accident. I didn't kill that old guy."

"You killed Bonnie Franklin?" Rylie asked, brows lifted.

He lowered himself into the seat and shook his head miserably. "I didn't mean to. She was hitchhiking, got some guy to drop her off. I think she wanted to stay overnight 'cause she didn't have the money. But this is my kingdom. I told her to get lost. And she wouldn't. So I started kicking her, and I smacked her. And she wouldn't go. She told me she was gonna call the police. And so I kept it up. And then she stopped moving." He sniffled and his hands shook. "I brought her out back of the restrooms and left her there. That's all. I didn't kill no man. My kingdom is peaceful, and he pointed a gun at me . . ."

He started to cry softly.

"Peaceful? You killed a woman," she said between gritted teeth. But something about him told her that this wasn't their man. Sure, he could've hitchhiked or stolen a car to commit the murders, but he was slovenly and greasy. He couldn't even keep himself clean. His getting away with Bonnie's murder was probably dumb luck, but the others . . .

It was something, at least. They might not have found their criminal, but they'd at least be able to get one killer off the streets. Rylie motioned to Michael to the side, to talk to him. "We'll have to get in touch with the state police and wait here until they come to take him into custody."

He nodded. "Guess it doesn't make sense to go to that other rest stop. This is clearly the one both victims stopped at."

50

"Yeah. But what about our case? Looks like we're at a dead end with that one. Unless you have any other bright ideas?"

He shrugged. "I think we need to dig deeper, Wolf. Like you said, there's something tying these cases together, and we just need to find out what it is. Eventually, the killer's going to slip up."

At that moment, a bone-deep exhaustion swept over her. She hadn't realized it until that moment, but they hadn't slept in over twenty-four hours. "All right. Let's get this guy taken care of, and then we'll dive back into the files."

She looked out toward highway I-86 and bit her lower lip. Eventually, maybe the killer would slip up and give them the clue they needed. But how many more people would have to die before he did?

CHAPTER TEN

An hour later, after the Billings Police came and took Ethan into custody, Rylie and Michael stood in the conference room of the Billings Police Department, trying to decide their next move.

Andy Boswick, Chief of the Billings Police Department, had been thankful for their help involving the cold case of Bonnie Franklin's murder, but he'd also seemed a little reserved. Like he didn't want them around. Rylie was used to police departments reacting in one of two ways—either they were glad for the help, or they resented the intrusion. Boswick, unfortunately, seemed to be the latter.

The slight-framed man, who was baby-faced except for an exceptionally large dark mustache, hovered in the doorway as they stood around the conference table, the information from the files spread out before them. Michael had an old map in his glove compartment, and now they stood in front of it, trying to track the movements of each of the three victims.

"We looked into the murder of Nick Costas," he said as Rylie drew a red line down his possible route.

"And?" Michael asked.

Boswick shrugged. "Never found anything. Don't think you will, either. Probably just a transient, passing through. That's what you get on those interstates."

"And that's what you thought about the murder of Bonnie, right? It was some transient?" Rylie said, not looking up from the map. "When he was right under your noses, the entire time. He hadn't even left the rest area."

Boswick gnashed his teeth. "We interviewed him. He came out clean."

"Hmm," Rylie said.

"Look," the Chief said stepping inside. "I'm having a meeting here at four. I need this room. Will you be out by then?"

Michael checked the time on his phone. "We hope to be. In the meantime, maybe you can help us out with this?" he said, offering that olive branch. He was so good at making peace, when Rylie was the one who usually stirred things up. "You know the area around here better."

"I do," he said, coming forward and looking at the map as Rylie drew a yellow line, indicating the drive of Neez Ramirez from his cabin on the Canadian border. "You really think there's two murders connected to the same killer? Based on what?"

"Three," Rylie said. "That's what we're trying to find out."

"I've never even heard of—" Boswick sifted through the papers. "This one was strangled. This one stabbed, and he wasn't anywhere near I-86. Only thing that seems to connect them is that they aren't among the living."

"We think there must be something. Something they all did. Someplace they all stopped, possibly," Michael said. "That's why we found Ethan. We thought they'd all stopped at that rest area."

Rylie pointed to the routes. "Can't be though, now that I look at it. Neez might have stopped there, but that rest stop is north of Billings. Nick Costas wouldn't have stopped there. Neither would Bobette Langdon, if she was coming all the way from . . . here." She marked an X by Sioux City. "That's really out of the way."

"So you think all three of them stopped at the same place and had an altercation with the same psycho?" he asked, stroking his clean-shaven chin. "Good luck with that. You got about five-thousands places between Billings and here." He pointed to the spot where Nick Costas, the closest one to Billings, was found.

"Yeah. We might need more manpower for this," Rylie suggested, eyeing the man.

He snorted. "Don't look at me. We're already stretched thin as it is, due to budget cuts, and I'm not sending a single one of my men on this half-assed wild goose chase. That's what it is, if you ask me. Call the Montana Highway Patrol."

Then he sauntered out.

Michael sidled next to her. "Looks like we're on our own."

"Wonderful man," she grumbled, looking after him. "Seriously, who gave him a badge? We solve one of his biggest cold cases, and this is how he thanks us?"

Michael shrugged. "Can't really blame him. There's a lot of territory to cover between Billings and the first crime scene."

She glared at him. He was always playing devil's advocate. Couldn't he just agree with her, for once? Then she sighed. "I guess.

We should call the Highway Patrol and see if they can help, if they have any resources they can lend us."

"Yeah. I'll get on it," he said, picking up his phone.

As he made the call, she leaned over the map and looked at the lines. All of the lines seemed to jumble in her head. Maybe Boswick was right; this was a wild-goose chase. If it was, then maybe they just needed to concentrate on what they had the most information for.

Michael ended the call. "They told me to send over a list of what we're looking for, and they'll put out an APB so their officers can check out any suspicious activity on the highway."

She nodded. "We're getting too distracted by the details of the other cases. I think what we need to do is work on this." She pointed to the photograph of Bobette Langdon. "Focus on the most recent case, since we have the most hot information on it. Let's find out where they impounded her car and check that out for any evidence the police might have missed, and try to really focus on these details. Forget the others, for now."

"If you say so," he frowned. "So where is her car impounded?"

Rylie gave him a sour look.

He picked up his phone. "Right. I'll figure it out."

She smiled and while he made the call, Rylie packed up all their files, then gathered them into her arms.

As she finished, Michael ended the call. "It's at an impound lot in a place called Columbus."

"All right. Let's go," she said, heading for the door.

Before she could step out, Boswick appeared, frowning. "Like I said, I need this room for—"

"Help yourself," she said, brushing past him. "We're all done here. Thank you for your help."

CHAPTER ELEVEN

Rylie watched the mountains in the distance, melting into the cloudless blue sky, as Michael drove west, toward Columbus. She was thinking about Bobette, alone, driving out to meet her twin sister.

She couldn't help but feel a pull at her heartstrings when Bambi spoke about her dead sister. Though Maren wasn't officially dead, she'd long since realized it would've been better if she was. That way, she'd know. There'd be no "what if?" Every time she went into a supermarket, she couldn't help but wonder if every woman around Maren's age was her long-lost sister. Every time, she'd gotten her hopes up, just a bit.

Rylie and Maren had been close, but toward the end, she'd begun pulling away, getting more interested in boys and make-up and things that didn't interest Rylie. Still, she'd been protective, and kind, helping with her homework and things like that.

Rylie never really got to see who Maren would become as an adult. What she would do with her life. It left a big question mark, yet another "what if." What if she was out there, somewhere, an adult, doing the things she'd dreamt of doing? Bambi, at least, had gotten a lot of years with her sister, before her tragedy.

"I think you're right," Michael said suddenly, breaking her out of her trance.

She glanced over at him. He side-eyed her, a curious look on his face.

Inwardly, she groaned. Why had she told him about Maren? It had only created a massive gap of awkwardness between them. Now, when he looked at her, she always thought she saw pity.

"Right about what?"

"About the third victim. That's where we need to concentrate," he said, pulling off at the exit for Columbus.

The impound yard was down the street from the gas station where she'd been murdered, about three miles off. They passed a few broken-down businesses, the remnants of a ghost town that looked to have closed down years prior. The impound lot was surrounded by a chain-link fence, a small, brick building attached to it. They parked between a couple of tow trucks, and when they stepped out, it looked like there was nothing around but yellow, grass-covered hills, for miles.

They went into the office of the impound yard and the clerk there gave them the key to the car and led them out to the yard. There were only a few vehicles in the lot that weren't coated in a thick layer of brown dust. Bobette Langdon's was one of them. It was an old-model Toyota Camry, silver.

Rylie went to the driver's side door and opened it, peering inside at the place where the poor woman had been murdered. She imagined the blonde woman, fighting for her life, struggling to breathe, all the while being choked to death by the killer.

Leaning in, she noticed the scuffs on the steering wheel and wondered if that was from the struggle. She also saw what looked like a burgundy red stain, in the footwell of the passenger seat. It looked like something had spilled there. She leaned forward, sniffing the scent of wine. Miniscule bits of glass were buried in the carpet. Were those tiny glass shards? Like from a broken wine bottle? The cashier at the convenience store had said that she'd bought a bottle of wine. She must've broken it during the struggle.

Across from her, Michael opened up the passenger-side door and peered inside, opening the glove compartment to a tiny travel umbrella and the car's registration paperwork. "See anything?"

She reached in and opened the console, but there was nothing inside. "Nope."

Squatting, she shone the flashlight from her phone under the seat, and then knelt on the seat and arced it around the back seat. It was pretty clean for a vehicle as old as it was, though it was likely that much of the contents of the car had been taken in by the Highway Patrol as evidence.

Michael began to reach into the seat cushions for anything that might have fallen between them, and she did the same. At first, she sighed in defeat, but then her fingertips scraped against something. It was a piece of paper.

"Wait. . . I think I found something," she said, thrusting her fingers in deeper so she could try to drag it out. After a few attempts, she managed to work it out of the place it had been wedged into. She pulled it out and stared at it.

"What is it?" Michael asked.

She read it over, paying careful attention to the date and time stamp. "A receipt. For the Blinking Star Diner in Laurel. You know where that is?"

He shook his head.

"Looks like she had the chili and a glass of water at around nine o'clock on the night she was killed. I don't remember hearing anything about her stopping there in the report, do you?"

"Nope. But nobody knew."

"Until now . . .," she said, something niggling at her mind. It was something to do with a detail she'd heard that sounded familiar. "We went over the credit card records. Nothing showed for—"

"Unless she paid cash."

"Right. Unless she paid cash." Suddenly, something popped into her mind. "Hey. Wait. Neez's son said something about a diner, didn't he? "

Michael stared blankly. "I don't know. The son I talked to told me to go to hell."

"No, wait, I know where I heard it," she said excitedly. "Sabina, Nick Costas's fiancé. She told me that Nick had stopped at a café and eaten something, and he was afraid he was going to have the runs, and have to stop at every rest stop, since the food was so bad. He was supposed to call her when he reached Yellowstone. But that's why when he didn't call her, she thought maybe he'd gotten sick and that was what had delayed him."

"She thought he had the runs?" He raised an eyebrow, amused. "Touching story. Let me guess. You want to go and check out this diner?"

"Only seems natural. We should check the car out first, but after that, don't you think we should?"

He shrugged. "I'll be honest, I've never said no to visiting a diner. But after that story, I might decide to pass on an early dinner."

*

It made sense why people would stop at the Blinking Star. It was the only non-fast-food restaurant for at least fifty miles. Not only that, but it was right off the highway, and there were at least a dozen billboards, on the way to Laurel, advertising it. The photographs on the ads even made Rylie hungry—big stacks of pancakes, steaks with mashed potatoes, golden fried chicken and biscuits.

57

But when they arrived at the diner, the appearance was a little underwhelming. The sign for it was almost bigger than the place itself. It was a rundown old place with a yellow roof, wagon wheels on the outside walls, and a bunch of barrel planters outside with nothing in them but dirt.

"That place just looks like it serves bad food," Michael observed.

"No one says you have to eat," she said, getting out of the car.

He joined her as she climbed the wheelchair ramp to the entrance. "But I'm hungry."

"Aw. See if they have any oyster crackers. You should be safe with those." As she reached for the door, she noticed a handwritten sign, and pointed it out to him. *CASH ONLY! At this time, we do not accept credit card's or check's. THANK YOU!*

He stared at it, shaking his head. "I hate when people use unnecessary apostrophes. Big pet peeve of mine."

"I was talking about the fact that they only accept cash, Bris," she muttered, though she had an idea he was only playing dumb to get her riled. She held up the receipt. "The waitress's name is Vicki. We should try to sit in her section."

When they stepped inside, Rylie inhaled, hoping for the smell of good food. But she got the opposite. It smelled like old cigarettes and bacon grease. The woman at the cash register was ringing up another customer. She was wearing a checkerboard plaid blue dress, like Dorothy, her hair a sprayed blonde helmet on her head.

"Sit anywhere," she mumbled, barely looking their way as she thrust a couple of plastic-coated menus toward them and continued talking to the old man with the combover who was paying for his meal.

Rylie leaned forward to read the name sewn on the pocket of her dress, in elegant script: Vicki. "Uh . . .excuse me?"

The woman looked up.

"Where is your section? We'd like you for our waitress."

The woman looked surprised, and then smiled, flattered. "Well, guess my reputation precedes me," she said, to the laughter of the other men, waiting to pay. "Actually, Honey, all of that section there is mine."

"Thanks."

They took the menus and sat down at a table in the dining area. All the tables were wooden, country-style, with mismatched chairs, and there were paper placemats at every place setting. Rylie set the menu aside and looked at the placemat, advertising all kinds of local businesses, tapping her fingers on the table as she waited for the waitress to come over.

Michael opened the menu and scanned it.

She tilted her head at him. "I thought you weren't going to eat anything?"

"Wolf. I can't sit down at a place like this and open a menu and not order. It's physically impossible."

She sniffed. "Are you serious? How can you smell that . . . and have an appetite?"

"Smell what?" He sniffed the air, then shrugged.

"Forget it."

He pointed at the menu. "I'll just have a grilled cheese. You can't mess up a grilled cheese. That was the first thing I learned to make, as a kid. When I was nine."

"Knock yourself out," she said, not really paying attention. Vicki was still chewing the fat with some people sitting at the stools at the bar. Was she ever going to come over and take their order?

"Stop it."

She blinked over to Michael to find him staring at her suspiciously. "Stop what?"

"Stop being impatient. She'll be here when she gets done with those guys. Relax."

"This is a murder investigation. You don't relax in a murder investigation."

"Yeah, you do. You can. A few minutes isn't going to kill anyone." He pointed to the menu. "You better order something, too. I know how you feel about fast food."

It was true, she wasn't a fan of fast food, especially since that's what she'd been eating a lot of, since moving out east. There just hadn't been time for many home-cooked meals. She'd never even used the kitchen in her apartment in Rapid City. Plus, it was dinnertime, and she didn't really want to have to stop later. She rolled her eyes and grabbed the menu, wondering what she could have that wouldn't get her sick.

As she did, the waitress finally came over and dropped two glasses of cloudy water in front of them, the contents sloshing onto the table. "Hey, you guys," she said, sounding a little more friendly, now that they'd flattered her by wanting to be served by her. "You have a chance to look at our menu? Our soup today is the split pea and our special is chipped beef."

Michael licked his lips. "I'll have a Coke, the soup, and the special then, heavy on the gravy."

Rylie winced. What happened to the grilled cheese? If he didn't want to get sick, that probably wasn't the way to do it. She gained three pounds, just thinking about that dinner. "I think I'll just have the chef's salad. Hold the egg. And the ham. And the onion. French dressing."

"You got it," she said, sauntering away.

"Vicki. Before you go," Rylie said before she got too far, reaching for her credentials as the woman stopped in her tracks. Rylie flipped them to the woman, whose mouth made an O. "Can we ask you a few questions?"

"FBI?" She was still staring at the badge. She looked mesmerized, like she wanted to touch it. "What? Why? Is that a real FBI badge? Are both of you—"

"Yes, we're here for a case, and we think you might be able to help," Michael explained.

She shook her head. "I don't think so. I don't know anything about a case. I've never even heard anything about the FBI coming all the way out here, in the middle of nowhere. We don't have very much going on for you fancy FBI agents to investigate."

"You'd be surprised," Rylie said under her breath, as Michael opened his phone and brought up the picture of Bobette.

"Do you remember her?" he asked.

She stared at it. "No . . . should I?"

"She might have been here the night before last," Michael said. "Around nine o'clock?"

"Nine? Hmm . . .," she laughed. "By then I've been on my feet for ten hours. I work from eleven until ten, most nights. By the end of the night, I'm dragging. Everything's a blur."

"I understand," Michael said with an encouraging smile. Rylie could already tell he was working his magic on her, like he worked on every female, because Vicki, despite being old enough to be his mother, was blushing. "She ordered a chili? Sound familiar?"

Vicki shook her head. "Sorry, Honey."

"That's okay," Michael said, as Rylie went through her own phone.

She pulled up the photograph of Nick Costas and presented it to the waitress. "What about this individual? Do you know him? This was almost a week ago, probably--"

"Yes!" The woman's eyes lit up. Then she rolled them to the ceiling. "Oh, God, do I remember that one! I told myself when he left

60

that if I ever saw his face again, it would be too soon. Total nightmare!"

Rylie smiled. Now they were getting somewhere. "How so?"

She grabbed the chair next to Rylie and pulled it out, sitting down and getting herself comfortable, as if she had a long story to tell. "Well, it's like this. With that internet thing, people work from anywhere, nowadays. We've been getting a lot of transplants from the cities, wanting to live the simple life and moving out here to the country, ruining our way of life. This kid was one of them. Nasty bit of work."

"What did he do?" Michael asked.

"He came in here and asked for something vegan, and we tried to get him a salad, but he didn't like that we couldn't verify it was cruelty free," she said with a sigh. "I had no idea what he was talking about, ranting on and on about animals in cages and our duty to be kind to the planet and stuff like that."

"Really?" This sounded like a far cry from the Nick Costas his fiancé had called *a good guy, a helpful guy.* He sounded like a nightmare. Of course, in Rylie's experience, it wasn't unusual for a wife or fiancé to have an entirely different opinion of a person than what everyone else had of him.

"Oh yes," she said, slamming both hands down upon the table. "I wanted to turn him away but Topher—he's our manager— told me I should just serve him as best we could. So I did. I brought him our salad and the soup he asked for."

"And?"

She snorted. "He said it was trash." She paused, for effect. "Trash! Can you believe that? I came up and asked him how everything was and he told me this place was trash and he was going to write a bad Yelp review. I had to tell him we had no idea what that even was, and he got angry. He said he wasn't going to pay and started causing a scene, throwing the menu down and rattling his silverware."

"What happened then?" Michael said, clearly amused by this story.

"Exactly what you'd think." She shrugged. "Topher came to the front and asked him to behave, and when he didn't, when he continued to disturb everyone else who was eating, Topher escorted him to the door. He never did pay for his food."

"Sounds like something was really bothering him," Michael observed. "I don't know many sane people who'd throw that kind of fit just over some bad salad."

"Right?" She shook her head. "I don't know. All those transplants coming around here, bringing their mental illness with them. That's what I told Topher it was. Mental illness. They're all stressed because all they do is sit in front of their idiot boxes. But not the TV. It's the new idiot box— their phones."

Rylie made a mental note of that. *Was something upsetting Nick Costas when he stopped at the Blinking Star Diner?*

She asked, "This Topher . . . where is he? Do you mind if we have a few words with him?"

"Not at all, Honey," she said, standing up. Though Rylie had asked the question, she said it mostly to Michael, her new crush. She even put her hand possessively on his shoulder, patting it. "He's right out back, in the kitchen. Let me put your order in and I'll tell him to come on out in a jiffy."

"Thank you," she said, exchanging a glance with Michael. He might've been excited about getting his heart-attack on a plate, but she was excited for another reason. She felt like they might finally be getting somewhere . . . maybe this diner was the connection they were looking for.

CHAPTER TWELVE

Rylie finished her salad and started drumming her fingers on the table, again.

"What do you think this diner manager, Topher, is going to tell us?" Michael asked, polishing off every last bite of his giant chipped beef platter. It had looked unappetizing, smelled even worse, and yet, her partner had no problem wolfing it down. He'd even said the split pea soup had "tasted funny," and yet that hadn't stopped him from sucking down every last drop.

"I don't know. But we have to interview him."

"Yeah. But if he was in the back for most of it, it's likely his story will be the same or less than Vicki's." He reached into his back pocket for his wallet and pulled out a couple of twenties.

"You're saying we shouldn't interview him?"

He swallowed his last remaining bit of dinner. "No . . . we should . . . obviously."

"There's something about this place," she said, looking around. Yes, it looked like an ordinary greasy spoon, but there was something else to it. "The fact that Nick Costas ate here, and Bobette Langdon ate here . . . it feels like more than a coincidence that they both had their last meals at this place."

"Maybe. Or maybe we're just reading too much into it. Like you saw, it is the only restaurant around for miles."

That was true. But she wasn't about to drop this lead quite yet.

Rylie twisted back and forth, craning her neck to see into the back. "Maybe I'm just being impatient again. But that he hasn't come out to talk to us yet is a little concerning, don't you think? It's been forty minutes."

"Concerning . . . you mean, suspicious?" he asked, checking the back, himself.

She nodded.

"No. It's the dinner rush. He's probably busy."

It wasn't crowded in the restaurant, but more tables were occupied now, and Vicki and the other waitresses kept rushing back and forth with trays of platters, for the waiting customers. But the cook had already come out twenty minutes ago to talk to another customer, and they'd asked Vicki if that was Topher. She'd told them no, that Topher "had been tied up."

"I don't know what's keeping him!" she said to them, every time she passed their table, in addition to making sure they had enough to drink.

Rylie sighed. "Topher's not the cook, though. It's not like he's the one pushing these orders through. I mean . . . he can't take time out to talk to us for five minutes? I mean, we are the FBI."

"Don't be an elite snob."

She glared at him. "That's not what I'm saying. I'm saying that if I had a list of things to do and the FBI came to ask me some questions about a murder, I don't think I'd be able to get anything done until I spoke with them. Call me overly curious. Am I wrong?"

"No, you're probably right," he admitted, looking to the back again. Then he pushed his plate away, motioned to Vicki, and slumped in his chair, gazing out the window.

Suddenly, he straightened. "That's interesting. Does that look bizarre to you at all?"

"What?"

She turned in her seat and followed his line of vision to a man, who was crouching behind the dumpsters, like he wanted to make himself as small as possible. His eyes shifted back and forth, from the diner to the parking lot, to the diner again, as if he was checking to make sure the coast was clear.

"Hmm, I'd say," Rylie said, inching closer to the window. "What do you think he's up—"

Suddenly, he sprang from his crouched position and ran for the parking lot, his tie flapping over his shoulder. He was a slim man with a slight build, wearing a short-sleeve dress shirt, despite the chill in the air.

"Hell. Now, if I'm not mistaken," Michael said, throwing his napkin down and rising to his feet, making a move to the exit. "Our manager friend Topher is trying to run away from us."

"You really think. . .," she asked, but it was a silly question. From the looks of it, Michael was right. That was exactly what it appeared to be. "But why would he . . .?"

She didn't have to wonder. *He'd only make a break for it if he had something to hide.*

"Get him!" she shouted, but she didn't have to.

Michael was already taking off like a bolt of lightning for the front door, with Rylie at his heels.

CHAPTER THIRTEEN

By the time Rylie got outside, the manager was already in his car, backing out. "Stop him!"

Michael was standing behind his car, trying to act as a barrier to get him to stop, but the crazed man tore out of the space anyway. Michael twisted to the side at the last minute, narrowly evading his car, and reached for the door handle.

As he did, he shouted, "Stop! Stop, dammit!"

From the look in his eye, he had no intention of stopping.

Still, she had to try. As the man lurched the car into drive, she stood in the center of the roadway, mere yards away from his front bumper.

His eyes met hers. She held them. "Stop."

He revved the engine and gesticulated wildly. She could hear him shouting, despite his windows being closed. "Get out of the way!"

She shook her head, reached for her gun, and pointed it at him. "Step out of the car," she said calmly, enunciating each word so he could understand.

He shook his head.

Rylie kept the gun level at him and narrowed her eyes, to show him she wasn't budging.

By that time, Michael had come around the driver's side and stood at his door, trying the handle. It was locked. "Open the door," he said.

The man looked from Michael, to Rylie, and back again. Finally, he slammed both hands on the steering wheel, threw the car into park, and cut the engine.

The second the door was unlocked Michael opened it, grabbed him by the shoulder, and hefted him out of the car, slamming him up against the side of it. "Topher?"

He nodded. "Yeah."

"Funny we should meet like this. What're you running from, pal?" he asked as he patted him down for weapons. "We told Vicki we just wanted to talk to you."

"I don't have anything to say," he mumbled, wincing.

"You could've told us that, and we wouldn't have had to make this kind of scene," he said, motioning with his chin toward the diner. Sure enough, several of the waitresses and customers were watching with great interest.

He groaned as Rylie snapped handcuffs on him. "I don't have anything to say," he repeated.

"Why don't we go inside, where we can be more comfortable, and we'll see about that?" Rylie said, nudging him toward the restaurant.

*

Five minutes later, they were sitting in a shabby little office beside the kitchen. It smelled even worse, here, like bacon grease mixed with cleaning supplies. Topher's desk was covered with papers and a giant computer that was so old, it had a floppy disk drive. The shelves behind his desk were piled with giant binders with the years on them, dating back to 1980.

"So, friend," Michael said, scooting his chair closer to the man and fixing him with a hard stare. "Tell us. Why did you run?"

He looked up at the wall, away from them, as if pretending they didn't exist.

Rylie moved closer. "We can make this easy, or we can make this hard. Your choice."

He met her eyes. "I told you, I don't have anything to say."

"And that's why you were sneaking out? That doesn't look very good for you, dude," Michael said, grabbing a piece of paper off the desk and reading through it, then tossing it down. "Innocent people don't run from the FBI. So naturally, we're suspicious. What do you know about the murders?"

His eyes widened. "Murders?"

Rylie nodded. "What did you think this was about?"

He coughed. "Not murders. Vicki just told me there were a couple of people with badges who wanted to talk to me. I . . ." He leaned in, as if imparting a secret. "I just thought you were the guys from the health board. We're . . . well, we're in violation."

"How is that?" Michael asked.

"The health inspector came a month ago and told us we couldn't open until we fixed about a hundred things. Okay, so we've been serving expired foods and everything isn't the cleanest. The place is old. But I can't not open. My family depends on this place. So I

67

thought I could get everything taken care of before he came back. But it's been slow going. And . . . well, let's just say we shouldn't be operating. So I thought you were the guys, come to haul me away."

Rylie noticed Michael's hand go to his stomach. He looked a little sick. "Expired foods?"

"Yeah, well . . .a couple people blame us for food poisoning and you think it's the end of the world." He shrugged.

Michael's face turned greener.

"Should've went for that grilled cheese, huh?" she murmured to him, before looking at the manager. "So you know nothing about the two victims?"

"Victims? No, I swear," he said, shaking his head vehemently. "You can ask Vicki. I spend most of my time in my office. I might be called if someone asks to see me, in which case I might have to escort them to the door."

"And did you?"

He nodded. "I escorted a man to the door a couple weeks ago. Complainer. Even after I told him we'd comp the meal. But once he left, I never saw him again. I swear."

She stared at him, trying to decide if he was telling the truth. He sounded earnest, but she wasn't going to let him go that easily.

"Hey," he said, holding up a finger. "I remember that night. After I had words with him, I was feeling so bad I went to the Wagon Wheel. I was there all night. I got, uh, drunk, and well, the police had to come. I spent the night in jail. You can ask them. I was there."

"Which jail?" Michael asked.

"Billings. Downtown. Just call them up."

Rylie sighed. That meant another dead end.

She looked at Michael, who stood up and pulled out his phone. "All right."

Topher stared at them. "What's going to happen?"

"I'm going to call the board of health and see what they want to do. They might bring you in, they might not. It's up to them. Either way, this place is going to be closed for a while," he said, bringing the phone to his ear.

Rylie nodded and stepped out of the room, into the kitchen. Another false alarm. And yet she couldn't fight the feeling that it was quite a coincidence that two of the victims had eaten here. What else was there?

She yawned and looked out at the rapidly darkening sky. Night was on its way, and it was probably time to call it a day and start back up, in the morning. She hated to stop at all, but her eyes were crossing. They hadn't slept in a long time.

Maybe the answers would come to her after a good night's sleep.

CHAPTER FOURTEEN

They were quiet as they drove west on 86, toward Bozeman. Michael stared out at the star-heavy sky as he drove, trying to concentrate on the case before them.

His mind kept going to other things, though.

Rylie, however, was laser-focused on the murders. She usually was. It was impressive, considering her background. He wished he could be the same.

She shifted uncomfortably in her seat and grabbed her phone. "I'll call the Montana Pines and reserve our rooms. Just in case."

"Good idea," he said. His stomach had been aching ever since he swallowed that last bite of chipped beef. It'd only gotten worse when they'd gone into the back and he'd seen the condition of the kitchen. He was pretty sure he spotted a dead cockroach, there. Now, his stomach was rumbling non-stop.

But that was nothing compared to turmoil going on inside his head.

They were dead. They were all dead. Covered in blood. And she was gone.

His partner had gone through hell, just like he had. And yet she'd been able to tell him about it. He hadn't told anyone about his own skeletons . . . he refused to. He buried his head in the sand, joking to hide the pain whenever anything struck too close to the bone.

She'd bared her soul to him. It only made sense that he come clean to her, as well.

And yet, he couldn't.

Not yet.

Rylie ended the call and let out a muffled curse. "They don't have any rooms open."

He looked over at her, and for a second, he'd forgotten what she was talking about. Oh, right. The hotel for the night. "What? Are you kidding? That big place?"

"Yeah. I knew we should've reserved rooms when we were there earlier today."

They were driving past a sign, listing the various amenities at the next exit. Gas? Check. Food? Check, a McDonald's. Accommodations?

Big fat nothing.

This could be a problem.

"Oh, great," she muttered. "What if there's no place to stay at all tonight?"

He shook his head. "No. Remember? That one at the Columbus exit?"

She glared at him. "The one that was nearly burned to the ground? You can't be serious."

"Come on. That old lady, Henny, was nice."

She folded her arms over herself. "I think I'd rather sleep in the truck."

"You can. But I'll sleep in a nice warm bed."

"With about a million bed bugs, I'll bet."

He might've told her that they could drive all the way on to Bozeman. There'd definitely be another, nicer hotel in that town, ever since it'd become the bougie playground for the rich. But that'd be another three hours of driving, and he really didn't think his stomach could last that long. Sweat dampened his forehead, despite the cold air he had blasting through the vents.

"Are you all right?" she asked him as he tilted the vent so more cold air would hit his face.

"Yeah, sure," he said, pointing to the exit for Columbus.

She shrugged. "You're the driver. If you must stop, then stop."

He navigated to the ramp and exited. The old Super Montana Mo-Tel loomed there, looking somehow worse than the last time they'd visited it.

It'll be fine for you. You slept on a dirty basement floor in a frat house in school, he thought.

But for Rylie? That was another question entirely. She was far from a prima-donna, but everyone had their limits.

He paused at the end of the ramp, but then his stomach growled like a living thing was trying to fight its way out.

"It'll be fine," he said, mostly to reassure himself. "If we don't get too comfortable, we can get an early start tomorrow, right?"

"Trust me, I won't."

This time, though, there were a few cars in the lot. He pulled into the parking lot, closest to the office, and the two of them went inside. He was expecting that old lady, but there was a younger guy behind the counter, reading a copy of *Popular Mechanics* Michael had seen on the coffee table, the last time they were there. He had dark scruff and long hair sticking up in all directions, and looked as though he'd just gotten in from a hard night of partying. "Need a room?" he said, yawning.

"I thought Henny was the only one who worked here?"

He shook his head. "You think that old bat can work here twenty-four hours a day? She has helpers. I'm her son. I work here some nights when she's not feeling well." He gave him a once-over. "Who are you?"

"We were here earlier, interviewing her about the murder across the way."

The kid snorted. "Yeah? What are you, police?"

Rylie said, "FBI. You know anything about it?"

"Nah. I don't live around here. I was in the trailer park, down near Laurel. That's where I live. I got a wife and kids there. But Henny told me all about it. Figures, the one night exciting shit goes down, and I miss it." He laughed. "Hell, if you were interviewing her as a witness, you must be pretty hard up. The lady's off her rocker."

Michael looked back at Rylie, who shrugged. It seemed like there were no good witnesses to Bobette Langdon's murder.

"So . . . do you need a room or don't you?" He prodded, holding up a key attached to a blue plastic keychain. "If you do, you'd better snatch it up because it's the last one I have left."

He nodded, reaching for his wallet, but froze suddenly when his words registered.

"Wait. You only have one?" Rylie asked.

"Yep. Crazy busy night. We're usually not like this, but . . ."

"Are you sure? You don't—"

"Look." He was clearly getting annoyed. "I should know how many rooms we have. We used to have twelve, until the fire. Now we have seven. We have six guests staying in the motel. If elementary school has served me right, that leaves . . ." He counted on his fingers.

"Yeah, yeah, yeah. Got it." Michael turned back and looked at her. "We could—"

"It's fine," she said, shaking her head. "You take it. I can sleep in the car."

"Are you kidding? No. I can't let you do that. I'll sleep in the—"

"I don't need chivalry. Your truck is nice, and I'm smaller than you. I'll be fine."

72

Michael shook his head slowly. He'd fight her on this, as long as it took. It was wrong to let her sleep outside, especially since someone had just been murdered in their car, right across the street. Sure, Rylie could hold her own, but . . . he wasn't that big of a jerk. "No, I—"

"There are two double beds in the room," the clerk said, dangling the key in front of them. "If that makes any difference."

Michael eyed Rylie, trying to gauge what she was thinking. But that was the thing about Rylie Wolf. She had a great poker face. He never knew whether she was pissed off or happy. Actually, she really only showed one emotion—intensely passionate. Like, she wanted everything done yesterday.

"Look, guys—you're about to lose the room," the man said, pointing to a couple of headlights that were flashing in the distance. A car was heading off the ramp, coming closer to the motel's lot. He snapped his fingers. "I don't got all day. Either crap now or get off the pot."

"I guess it's fine, if there are two double beds," she said, snatching the key and heading outside, leaving him to pay.

"Cash or credit?" the clerk said.

Michael handed over his credit card, had it swiped, and went outside. By the time he got out there, the clerk had already turned on the NO in front of the VACANCY sign out front. Oddly enough, the other party was nowhere to be found. They'd probably taken one look at the place and run in the other direction.

Michael wondered if, when he saw the room, he'd wish they'd done the same.

As he reached the last door in the strip, his stomach growled again. He needed to go across the street and get some Pepto. But he went inside instead and found Rylie standing next to the bed nearest the restroom, looking at it in disgust. She was still holding her bag, as if she was afraid that the cockroaches and other vermin would devour it if she dared to set it down.

Everything was rust-colored, and there was actual shag rug on the ground, but it was so matted in places that it was almost threadbare. The television was chained to the wall. Everything smelled like mothballs and cheap pine air freshener.

She reached over and peeled the comforter off the bed. "Most hotels only wash comforters once a week," she explained, tossing it in a corner. "I bet this place *never* washes them."

He looked around. He could practically see the years of filth, piled up on every surface. "I think you're probably right."

She inspected the sheets themselves, especially near the headboard, probably for bed bugs, then gingerly sat down on the edge of the bed and checked her phone. "You want to use the bathroom first?"

He shook his head. "You go on. I'm going to go across the street for a minute."

"Checking out the crime scene again?"

"No." If he didn't get that Pepto, he was not going to survive the night, with the way his stomach was feeling. "Can I get you anything?"

She grabbed her toothbrush and toothpaste from her bag and shook her head. "I'll probably be asleep when you get back. I'm so tired, I'll probably be snoring before my head hits the pillow."

*

When Michael did return, about a half an hour later, he felt much better, the Pepto doing its job. The lights in the main area were out, but Rylie had left the bathroom light on for him, the door a bit ajar so he wouldn't have to be stumbling about an unfamiliar room in the pitch black. He went to the bathroom, took a shower, put on fresh underwear, tried to gauge where his bed was so he'd be able to find it in the dark, and turned out the bathroom light.

Five steps at most, skirting around Rylie's bed, and he'd be there.

But he must've misjudged the distance, because he slammed his shin into the hard, pointed edge of the closest bed frame. The pain was immediate and breathtaking.

"Dammit!" he blurted, unable to keep it in as he hobbled to the bed and sat down. "Holy hell!"

Rylie rolled over in bed but said nothing.

The pain subsided. He sat on the edge of the bed, massaging it, and whispered, "Sorry."

She responded, which surprised him. "That's okay. Wasn't asleep anyway."

"Yeah? What happened to snoring before your head hits the pillow?" He climbed into bed and pulled up the sheets. A spring seemed to jab him, right between the shoulder blades. "These beds that bad?"

"No, it's not that. Well, it's a little of that," she admitted in the darkness. "But I'm also thinking about the case. About how the killer is choosing his victims."

"And?"

"And I still think he's going by convenience of proximity. Basically, they're in the wrong place at the time he wants to find a victim. It's the only thing that makes sense."

"Okay. I thought we agreed on that."

"Yeah, but I'm just saying that because our victims are entirely random, we should continue to concentrate on places, rather than the victims themselves. Narrow things down a bit by really drilling into their routes. If there's a place one of them stopped at, we should concentrate there and see if any of the others stopped there. Like here."

"Funny you say that," he said with a smile. "When I stopped in with Randy across the street at the convenience store, I asked if he'd seen either of the other two victims. But he hadn't."

"Oh." She groaned. "Great. That was my next move."

"Well, we'll think of something else. But yeah, it's something. It's good to know that it had nothing to do with the victims' backgrounds themselves. Ruling things out is just as valuable."

She rolled over in bed so he could tell she was facing him. "Yeah, but I hate spinning wheels, and that's what I feel like we're doing."

He chuckled. "It's only been a day."

"But the more we run back and forth over this highway, checking out landmarks and finding nothing, the more careless we're going to become. And then the killer might be able to act right under our noses, and we'd never realize it," she said.

He tried to search her out in the darkness. It sounded like she was speaking from personal experience. He didn't know what it was like to have gone one's entire life, knowing there was someone on the loose who'd snatched a member of her family away from her. "We're going to find this killer," he assured her.

She didn't say anything for a long time. Then she mumbled, "But what if we don't? A lot of killers get away."

Now, she was definitely speaking from experience.

"You don't understand," she added a moment later.

A long silence stretched between them, and he thought about telling her. But he couldn't. Instead, he simply said, "I understand more than you think I do."

She didn't say anything. Maybe she was already asleep. But tomorrow was a new day, and they'd probably spend it checking out establishments up and down the highway to see if any of the victims had stopped there. With any hope, they'd find a new lead.

CHAPTER FIFTEEN

The man sat in the driver's seat of his pick-up, smoking a cigarette on the side of the road.

Tonight, he was just outside of Wyola, Montana.

Airlia Birnbaum had quite the busy day. She'd spend much of the time hiking solo in Bighorn Canyon, only to get on the road, heading east, later that afternoon. She'd taken far too many selfies, posed near different natural landmarks, and she'd eaten a granola bar on a butte, staring out into the canyon below, probably wondering if this was how it would feel to be the only person alive.

Of course, she wasn't. She hadn't noticed him, creeping up behind her, keeping a safe distance.

She had seen him though, once, when they returned to the parking lot. Their cars were the only ones there. She'd gone past him, said, "Hey," and that was it.

Then she'd stopped at a diner off the beaten path, grabbed dinner, and headed back onto I-86.

Now, she'd just gotten a cottage at a place called True North, where they had a number of crappy little log cabins, scattered along the valley. He'd seen her go in through the gates, stop at the office, and then get back into her car and drive out toward the main utility road.

He pulled through the gates himself, wearing his clever disguise. It had never failed him before. People rarely paid attention to maintenance workers, and they didn't now. The night manager, who went outside to smoke a cigarette shortly after giving Airlia her key, didn't even look twice as his truck rumbled up the dirt road, looking for the little bug with the COEXIST bumper sticker.

He found it at the very back of the complex, backed up to a line of trees. She'd already gone inside and turned on the lights.

He parked his truck next to hers and climbed out, adjusting the collar on his dark blue coveralls, and grabbed his toolbox.

He climbed the two short steps to the cabin and knocked on the door.

"Don't need any housekeeping, just got in!" she shouted from inside.

"Not housekeeping. Maintenance," he called back.

She opened the door a crack and peeked out. Smart girl, she was using the chain. Even though the door was only open a sliver, he could see she'd changed out of her hippie outfit and was wearing nothing but a towel. "What? I didn't call for maintenance. And I was just going to--"

"I'm with the state, Ma'am," he said kindly, showing her his bogus credentials. "There's a problem with the water line. If you're wanting to use the water, I'll need to check it. Otherwise it's gonna be a not-so-pleasant shower for you. The hot water shuts off without notice."

"Oh," she said, grimacing. She clutched the towel tighter around herself. "Yes, I was planning to. Can you give me a moment?"

"Of course."

She closed the door, and he waited outside, scanning the area. It was a nice little cabin she'd chosen, here. There wasn't a single neighbor or prying eye nearby. That would make his work, and his escape, easy-peasy.

A moment later, he heard the chain slide out, and the door opened wider. Now, Airlia was wearing a big t-shirt that said, *Amnesty International* and boxer shorts, probably belonging to that Back Bay Boston boyfriend of hers. "This won't take long, will it?"

"Nope. I'll be in and out," he said with a smile as he stepped in. *But I'm sorry, that shower of yours is not going to happen.*

The room was actually very nice. Nicer than that dump she'd stayed at the night before. It had a giant double bed that was made out of hewn logs, covered in a crisp, homey patchwork quilt. The décor was animal horns of all sizes, and photographs of the nearest geological wonders. He paused there, looking around, until she cleared her throat, a little impatiently. "Bathroom's right there," she said, pointing and sitting down on the bed. "I put all my stuff on the counter. Let me know if you need me to move it."

"Nope, should be good," he said, proceeding into the restroom. Sure enough, her many toiletries were already lined up on the counter. She sure did use a lot of products to achieve that fresh-faced, hippie look. He placed the toolbox on top of the toilet lid and stared at his face in the mirror, priming himself for what was to come. *Calm her down. Keep her suspecting nothing.* He called, "You on your way out west?"

"Actually, no. Heading east. To Boston. My boyfriend lives there. We've been having a long-distance relationship for the past six months. It sucks," she said with a laugh.

He listened carefully, hearing canned laughter in the background, which changed to the sound of a reporter, droning on about the news of the day. So she'd turned on the television and was now surfing the channels.

He grabbed a pair of latex gloves and snapped them on. Reaching over, he ran the water, then grabbed a hammer from the toolbox and clanked it against a pipe beneath the toilet, so she wouldn't get suspicious. "That's nice. You were out on the west coast?"

"That's right. I just graduated with my master's from UC Berkley. Now I'm out of there. I can't wait to get back east. That's where I grew up."

"Congratulations," he said, though none of this was news to him. He couldn't wait. He needed to do this now. He reached into the toolbox and pulled out the long, curved blade.

Then he walked to the door of the bathroom.

Airlia Birnbaum was sitting at the chair near the dining set, watching the television. Her back was to him.

Perfect.

She must've caught his reflection in the screen of the television, because she started to turn. "You almost done in—"

Her eyes went wide at the sight of the knife in his hand. She opened her mouth to scream but by then, he'd lunged at her, wrapping an arm around her and covering her mouth with that hand. He tipped her head back and, as she struggled against him, pulled the blade easily across her pale throat.

She whined and whimpered for a moment, her arms and legs flailing, before she finally gave up and fell still. When he let her go, she toppled forward against the tabletop, spilling blood across its surface.

He smiled, adrenaline pumping through his veins, and let out a low, satisfied breath. So good. That felt so good. "I know what you did to her," he whispered, making sure it was the last thing she heard.

Turning toward the bathroom, he went to wash up, rinsing the blood from his knife and hands. As he gathered his things and prepared to leave, he looked up at his reflection. He looked strong, powerful, like he owned the world.

And he knew . . . he just knew . . . that she would be so proud of him.

79

CHAPTER SIXTEEN

Rylie woke up to the smell of something even worse than the normal wet, moldy smell of the room. It smelled a little like hot garbage.

She sat up in bed to find Michael, fully dressed in his suit and tie, pulling food out of a rumpled white paper bag. Two Styrofoam cups of coffee were set out at the table, too.

She blinked. She'd been having that same recurring dream, from the night of the murders. Hiding in that cramped spot in the back of the RV, listening to the sound of the rain and thunder overhead. This time, though, she'd dreamt that she was outside, the rain falling on her as she watched Maren get pulled away by two men in head-to-toe black. She was screaming, for Rylie.

She swallowed around the nausea that bubbled in her throat from the mere memory of the dream. "Look at you," she said with a smile, rubbing her eyes. "I must've been out. I didn't even hear you."

"You were. I didn't want to wake you. You looked like you needed it."

Was it late? She grabbed her phone. It was after eight. Since when did she ever sleep that long? "I guess I must've needed it. But we should get out as soon as possible. Let me just take a quick shower."

She came over and took a sip of the coffee. It was like hot sewer water. She swallowed with some difficulty and said, "Thanks for getting breakfast."

"If you can call it that. The motel doesn't have a continental breakfast."

"Imagine that," she said, inching closer to the table, a little embarrassed because she was wearing what she always wore to bed—an oversize FBI t-shirt. She unwrapped a grease-stained wax paper to find a squished English muffin with electric-yellow cheese and a white layer that might or might not have been an egg. "Where'd you get this?"

"Our friend Randy," he said, pointing across the street. "I figured we should probably eat now, since our food options are limited. It's not

81

like we can eat at the Blinking Star, after last night. I could've gotten you something else but—"

"This is fine," she said, taking a bite of the sandwich. It was absolutely tasteless, though the texture was right. She didn't care what she ate. She had too much on her mind. She gathered her clothes and rushed to the bathroom, speaking louder as she closed the door, trying to ignore the fact that Brisbane was right on the other side of it as she shed her clothes. "So, I was thinking."

"About the case?"

"Of course, about the case!" she shouted through the door as she turned on the water. It was actually warm, and there seemed to be good water pressure, which surprised her. Speaking louder, she continued. "What I was thinking was that since all of these cases seem to be happening in the area from Billings toward Wineglass, we really need to just go from place to place and show the photographs around."

He said something back, but by then she'd jumped in the shower and the sound of the running water drowned it out.

"It's going to take a long time, but there really aren't a huge number of exits on the road. Maybe if we can speak to the Highway Patrol, they'll offer to lend a hand . . ."

He said something else, but she couldn't hear.

"Hold on." She lathered up quickly, rinsed, and turned off the water. She wasn't one for long, hot showers that made her skin prune, but this was probably the shortest one in her personal record. It felt too strange, showering in the same hotel room as Brisbane, even if he was on the other side of the door.

As she toweled off, she said, "What were you saying?"

"I was saying that it would be better if we didn't have to go from place to place and if the people could come to us if they recognized any of the three victims."

"I know," she said as she pulled her shirt on and buttoned it, then finished pulling on her pants. She peered out to find him standing *right* on the other side of the door. As his eyes swept over her, she was glad she'd brought all her clothes into the bathroom. "But we don't want to create a panic by releasing the victims to the media, especially if we aren't one-hundred-percent sure that it's the same guy, doing all the killings."

"True. Kit would probably have our heads if we got the media involved, because they'd all come to her for answers."

82

She wringed out her hair and twisted it up into a bun on her head, then scuffed into her shoes. "But you're right. I wish there were any easier way. But if . . ."

It came to her right then, a solution so simple, so right in front of her nose, it was almost embarrassing neither of them had thought of it. "We have phone records, right, which indicates the calls they made, and when, . . . all except for Nick Costas, who didn't have a phone. But can't Beeker trace other things with their phones, even when they haven't made a call?"

"Yeah . . .," He let out a short laugh and smacked his thigh. "Yeah. Of course. Why didn't we think about that before?"

"I just wasn't thinking about it. But he has to have the answer. He can give us the exact routes each of them took, and we just have to see where it overlaps."

When she finished tying her shoes, she looked up to find him already on his phone, thumbs moving over in a text. He'd finished his sandwich, but hers was waiting. She took a big bite, excited for the information.

Michael looked up. "He said it would just be a few minutes, and he'll see what he can send over."

She sat on the edge of the bed. "This'll be good. If we can find that out, then we don't have to run around like chickens with our heads cut off, asking at every fast-food restaurant whether they'd seen them."

"Yeah." He sipped his coffee. "Ready to get out on the road? In the meantime, we could—"

His phone beeped. He looked at it.

"Son of gun, that was Beeker. The kid's fast."

He opened something up on his phone and stared at it, using his fingers to zoom in and out. Rylie, excited, squeezed next to him, trying to see. There were three lines, indicating the route each person had taken, much like the map that they'd drawn in the conference room, yesterday. She squinted. "Do they intersect? At all?"

"Well, they all followed the same route, on I-86, so of course they're all the same there. But it looks like, yeah . . .Bobette got off on the exit for the Blinking Star, just like we thought. Nick probably did, too." He tilted his head.

"But what's that? I don't—" She leaned in closer, trying to see. It was only when she realized she could smell his aftershave, that she realized she was almost sitting in his lap, their thighs brushing.

She sprang up as if launched from a cannon, grabbing it from his hand, then blushed. *A tad of an overreaction, huh, Rylie?*

"Hey." He snatched it from her. If he'd had any reaction to her being that close, he didn't show it. "Chill. I don't think either of us will be able to see anything if we keep fighting over it."

She glared at him. "Fine. What do you see?"

He looked closer. "Okay, so Nick and Bobette likely both got off at the Blinking Star diner exit. But it looks like this exit . . .Bobette Langdon got off on it . . ."

"Duh. She died here. This is where her cell phone was found."

He held up a finger. "But Neez Ramirez got off here, too."

"He did?" She straightened. "And Nick Costas? You think maybe he did, too?"

He shook his head. "I don't know."

She sighed. "Can I see, now?"

He handed it to her. "Knock yourself out."

"Thanks," she muttered, snatching it and viewing it. She'd hoped for a smoking gun, the one place all of them had stopped during their individual journeys. But since they only had records for two victims, there were a lot of them. She saw the rest stop Neez had stopped at, but other than that, his route was very similar to Bobette's. Bobette had gotten off at this exit, driven about a little, and then stopped at the convenience store.

"This is no help," she groaned, handing him the phone. "It's almost like they took the exact same route."

Michael threw up his hands. "I don't know. So does it make sense to go around, asking people if they'd seen the victims?"

She shook her head. "I think we should do as I was saying before. Concentrate on Bobette, since it's most recent. Try to get into her head, a little."

"And how do we do that?"

"Well . . . look at the route she took. She got off at this exit, and she went one way, then hung a U turn and went the other way . . . it looked like she stopped at this motel."

"Henny said she didn't stay here."

"Yeah, but she was in the parking lot, right? So either Henny's lying, or Henny doesn't remember, or . . . "

"Maybe she took one look at this place and said, hell no, I can't stay here," Rylie said. "If she did, I can't blame her. Plus, didn't Randy say she asked for the name of a hotel because she didn't want to stay at that place across the street?"

Michael nodded. "Okay. So what does that tell us?"

"It tells us that she was unsure. That something bothered her about this place. Maybe she saw someone who frightened her."

Michael gnawed on his lip. "What about that guy . . . Henny's son? Maybe he had something to do with it?"

She nodded. "Maybe. We didn't interview him. We should try to check him out, see if he knows anything else."

As they were gathering up their things to leave, her phone began to ring.

It was Kit, from the FBI. Usually, getting a call from the director would strike dread into her, Kit wasn't nearly as bad as her old director, Bill Matthews in Seattle. Kit, at least, wanted her to do well.

"Kit," she said to him, holding it up so he could see.

"She probably wants to check in."

"Probably," she said, but it was odd. They'd only been on the case a day. And though they'd made progress, Kit was far less meddlesome than Bill Matthews had been. She usually gave them breathing room and let them report back when there was something to report. She answered. "Hey, Kit, what's up?"

"Hi, Rylie. Are you still out in Montana?"

"Yep, we're heading out to follow a couple of leads right now. Still not much luck in trying to find a common thread, but--"

"Well, then, this might help you," she said, taking a deep breath. "It seems that a body of a young girl was found in a hotel room in Wyola. You know where that is?"

Wyola. Of course, she did. That was almost in her own backyard. Whenever she thought about that area, dread formed a pit in her stomach. There were so many nights, spent alone, after the death of her mom and sister. So many days when her father essentially abandoned her, to go off and drink. She'd sit at home in her bed and cry and cry, and she dreamed of escape. She'd spent so many hours making that plan, to sneak across the fence onto her neighbor Hal's property, steal one of his horses, and head out. Anywhere. She hadn't cared.

Which reminded her. Hal would be upset with her if her knew she'd practically gone past his ranch without stopping in to say hello. She'd have to rectify that, once the case simmered down.

"Yeah. It's close to the Wyoming Border," she said dismissively. She was more concerned about the body. "What happened?"

"She was murdered. It's one of those places with a lot of little cabins, all spread out. Supposedly it was pretty full last night. A maid went in to change out her towels and found her with her throat slit."

Strangling. Stabbing. Now a slit throat? She gritted her teeth and made eye contact with Michael, who was trying to listen in. She shook her head. "What makes you think this might be our guy?"

"It might not be. But you can look into it and make that determination. I'm having Beeker send you the details right now. Let me know what you find out."

"I will. Thanks." She ended the call and looked at Michael. "Another victim. Female. Throat slit at a cabin near the Wyoming border. They think it might be related."

"Geesh," he said, running his hands through his dark hair. "Change of plans, then?"

"Yeah. We'll have to interview Henny's son later. Let's get on the road and get down to this crime scene as soon as possible."

CHAPTER SEVENTEEN

It was a two-hour ride to Wyola, near the Wyoming-Montana border. Rylie watched the buttes and barren desert landscape give way to pine trees and lush, green forests. It brought back all sorts of memories from her childhood—watching the cattle graze on the long expanse of ranchland owned by her neighbor, Hal, going fishing with Maren and her dad in the creek outside their house, and then, after tragedy struck, stealing one of Hal's horses and riding as fast and as far away as she could, trying to escape.

When Michael put on his blinker and navigated off the highway, it stirred her from those thoughts. They passed a sign for the True North Luxury Cabin Rentals, just outside of Wyola. It was a well-kept, gated community, nestled among the pines . . . but it was huge. When she stood in front of the giant map posted in front of the office, she realized there had to have been at least a hundred cabins there.

"This place is huge," she said to Michael when he came out of the office.

"Yeah, come on. I just spoke to Officer Black of the Highway Patrol. He's going to take us back there. It's a ride so he said we should follow in the truck."

It was a ride. They drove at least a mile, weaving between the cabins, on many different dirt roads, until Rylie was sure they'd never find their way out. When they broke free of a line of cabins, they saw the chaos—several police cars and an ambulance were parked outside a smaller cabin, backed up to the woods.

"So it's that one," she murmured to herself, a chill going down her back.

"Uh-huh. It's a wonder the killer even got in here, with that fence around the place."

"I don't think the fence is much of a deterrent," she observed. Though it was high and looked sturdy and rather new, there was no security at the gate. "You saw it. People are going in and out the front gate all the time. It's kind of a madhouse. I bet he just waltzed in the front."

"But someone should have seen him. Don't you think?"

"Maybe. Maybe not."

She got out of the car and climbed up to the front porch, flashing her credentials to the police officers there. The officer who had led them there shook her hand. "Agent Wolf, I'm Officer Black. Thanks for being here. I was just telling Agent Brisbane that this is the first we've seen of anything like this in the area. The place is usually very quiet. It's a family place. I don't have to tell you that the owners and the guests are really concerned."

"Have you spoken with the guests in the nearby cabins?"

He nodded. "None of them saw much. Like I said, a lot of families. And they were playing an outdoor movie near the fire pit, on the other side of the complex. Most of them were of there."

"You spoke to the person at the front office?"

Officer Black nodded again. "Unfortunately, they have people coming in and out, to stay, and to eat at their restaurant. And they have over a hundred staff and maintenance people in here at any one time, and they don't have them sign in at the front desk. So it's hard to tell. They do have cameras, but we've gone over the surveillance footage and there isn't much to go on."

"We should get a list of the maintenance people who came in," she told him, though she wasn't sure what good that would do. If killer didn't have to register with anyone, he could've slipped in, unnoticed.

She stepped into the cabin and looked around. The crowd of police photographers and officers parted, and she saw the woman, sprawled across a table, her eyes open. She was pretty, with long blonde hair, her ears pierced with a number of studs. She was wearing a white t-shirt, now stained with brown blood, and boxers. "Details on the victim?"

"Airlia Birnbaum, twenty-three, just graduated from Berkley in California a few weeks ago. She was traveling alone. She picked up the key last night at around eight, and she must've been murdered sometime in the night." He held up the Massachusetts driver's license of a smiling girl with long blonde hair, in better times.

Rylie moved closer, looking for clues. If this was the work of the same killer, it was the first victim he'd killed who was travelling east. "The killer leave any prints or anything?"

"Nope. We thought we had part of a bloody fingerprint, but it was the victim's. Killer must've worn gloves."

Every time Rylie took in a crime scene, she always thought back to that day when she was nine. She was used to it, now, but it still made her stomach turn. Especially a young girl like this—she couldn't help but think of her sister. Airlia's blood was spilled everywhere—pooled on the table, soaking her blonde hair dark, but mostly . . . on the carpet around her. "No footprints in the blood at all?"

"Not a thing."

She looked back at Michael, who murmured, "That fits in . . ."

He didn't have to say more. He was right. It sounded like it could be their man. But if so, they were now almost two hours east of the easternmost point where the other murders had taken place. That meant that they now had a lot more ground to cover.

She nodded to Officer Black and turned to leave. She couldn't stay there a moment longer. "I've seen enough," she said, hurrying out of the place.

When she was outside, she sucked in cool breaths of mountain air and picked up her phone, dialing Beeker. "Hi, Agent Wolf, and how are you on this fine day?" he asked in greeting.

She rolled her eyes. He was teasing her for not being cordial, whenever she called him. But that was just her way. So she ignored him. "I need your help."

"That good?"

"Beeker . . .," her tone was low, warning.

"All right, all right, chill. What do you need help with now?"

"There's another victim. I need to know if you can track where they were, like the other ones. Can you?"

"You know I can. But I do need something."

"What, the phone number?"

"I don't even need that. What's her name?"

"Airlia Birnbaum."

"Airlia," he repeated at the same time. She could hear the computer keys in the background rattling, a sound almost always present when she spoke with him on the phone.

"Of Boston, Massa—"

"Got it," he said. They didn't hire him at twenty-one for nothing. "Phone number, last known address . . . she was living in California, huh? Geez. She was pretty."

"Can you just—"

"Yeah, yeah, yeah. Stand by. It's on its way."

He seemed to have had enough of her, because he took a line from her playbook and ended the call without saying goodbye.

She stood there, staring out over the porch railing. It was deceptively calm and quiet here, except for the occasional police officer, telling curious guests to keep away. Last night, this young woman had met her end in a hellish way, never expecting something like this could happen. It seemed so cruel, to die alone like this.

Michael came out a moment later. "Got the number of the boyfriend in Boston. The police have already called him. She doesn't have other family. So I thought I'd give him a call, see if he can shed any light on what she was doing."

"Hmm," Rylie said.

"And then I thought we should interview some more of the guests around the lodge." He scanned the area and the people milling about beyond the perimeter the police had set up with their cars. It was getting to be quite the crowd. "Should take a while. Sure are enough of them."

"Hmm."

"Hmm?" he parroted. "What is that supposed to mean?"

She shrugged. She had a hunch, a bit of intuition, which told her that was going down a rabbit hole that they'd never be able to get out of. "Just seems like a waste of time. The girl was traveling alone, so we know who she was. She was independently minded. But since there was no sign of forced entry, she let her killer in of her own free will, which suggests that either she knew the assailant—which is doubtful, since she's not from around here—or that he finessed his way in somehow. And all these people? Interviewing them could take ages, and we'd get very little usable information. It might only confuse things."

"So, we shouldn't?" He raised an eyebrow.

She shook her head. "No, we should. It's just—"

She paused. She felt tired. Tired of going through the same song and dance, only to glean nothing but crumbs, that might have absolutely nothing to do with the case.

"We should," she said with finality. "I think I just need another cup of coffee, first."

Her phone buzzed. The message she'd been waiting for, from Beeker. Eagerly, she opened it and looked at it, tracing the route with her eyes, looking for one thing in particular.

But when she saw it, she let out a disappointed breath. There was no sign she'd been at the Super Mo-Tel motor lodge, either.

Dammit.

She looked up to find Michael staring at her curiously. "I'll get the coffee?"

She nodded, psyching herself up for the interviews. It was going to be a very long day.

CHAPTER EIGHTEEN

"Rich! Get in here!"

Bill Matthews sat at his desk in the FBI's Field Office for the Analysis of Violent Crime in Seattle, feeling pissed. He'd woken up pissed, and it had only grown as he went through page after page of national news regarding the FBI's rising star.

Rylie Freaking Wolf.

He thought about that time, in this office, a month ago, when he'd given Rylie her walking papers.

"I think what you were doing was going against the rules. As usual," he'd said.

"Possibly. But the main objective was to catch the man, right? And I—"

"Catch the man, yes. Tear up half a mile of highway? The median's a wreck. They say it's going to cost millions of dollars to fix!"

She'd scoffed at him, completely insolent, as always. "To plant a few bushes? Come on—"

That was enough. He'd lunged forward and slammed his palms down on his blotter, showing her he meant business. "You deliberately disobeyed orders. What about calling for back-up?"

"My phone was dead," she'd said calmly.

"According to the police report, you slammed your government-issued vehicle into the side of his van."

"That's right. I had to stop him."

"You could've injured the victim!" he'd shouted at her. *"Not to mention that was another hundred-thousand dollars' worth of equipment you destroyed."*

"I didn't mean to. And I wouldn't have hurt the kid. I made sure to hit the front of the car—"

"But still, you put that child in danger."

"The Thompsons didn't see it that way. They were grateful to have him back. And he wasn't hurt. Not at all. He's spending his night at home, safe, in bed, instead of in a cage. So it all worked out."

He pointed a finger at her. "You're lucky it all worked out. The next time, you might kill someone, or yourself. You understand me?"

Rylie let out a sigh. "Yes. I understand."

He eyed her, not believing a word she was saying. "I don't think you do. I can't have you endangering others and yourself, destroying property, just on a whim. The FBI handbook exists for a reason."

"The handbook is a guideline."

He pounded the desk with a single fist. "It should be your bible! I don't want you doing a single thing unless you find it in the pages of that book. You got it?"

"I've got it," she said mock-pleasantly. She was mocking him.

His eyes narrowed. "Do you really?"

She fisted her hands on her hips. "What is that supposed to mean?"

He clenched his teeth. "Because I seem to remember bringing you in here to discuss this very thing, just last month. And the month before that."

"Yes, but—"

"But nothing, Wolf. Stop being so emotional! If you don't put your female emotions under control and get your act together . . ."

Something inside her seemed to snap.

She stepped forward and put both hands on his desk, leaning forward as if she was about to whisper something. But instead, she spoke at full volume. "Listen, you pretentious prick. You only got this job because your daddy needed someplace to put you where you'd stay out of trouble. You have no business being here. And you certainly don't have any business telling any of us how to do our jobs."

Then she turned on her heel and stomped out of the room, slamming the door behind her.

He couldn't believe the news, at first. That woman, who'd told him off in front of his entire group, had single-handedly shattered the relationships he'd been cultivating with the other agents on the floor. She'd efficiently and effectively undermined his authority, and he was still trying to get it back. Now, when his agents looked at him, he couldn't help thinking they felt the same: *You don't have any business telling us how to do our jobs.*

Not only that, but Rylie Wolf was reckless to an extreme. Always going against the grain and doing what she wanted to do, instead of following protocol.

That was the reason he'd gotten rid of her. As Unit Chief, it was not only important for him to protect his fellow agents, but the integrity of the unit itself. She took risks and there was only a matter of time before he had to answer for them.

Well, it was *one* of the reasons.

He wouldn't admit it, but a bigger reason was because she constantly undermined him, challenging his authority. She made no attempt to disguise her complete lack of respect for him. And for what? Nepotism? Yes, his father, Jerry Matthews, the Deputy Director, might have given him this job, but he'd earned it. He'd had to deal with a lot of shit in order to get here, and people like Wolf couldn't see that. Those years at Yale Law hadn't been a cakewalk, and that day at Quantico had been one of the hardest in his life.

So when he'd forced her out east, into the middle of nowhere, he'd thought—he'd hoped—it would be the last he ever heard of her.

He was wrong.

He gritted his teeth as he scanned another headline, this one from *USA TODAY: FBI Cracks Case of Second Mid-Western Serial Killer in a Month.*

His lip curled into a snarl as he scanned and saw her name in print. *"This area of the United States has simply been ignored by federal law enforcement, and smaller local police departments haven't had the manpower to adequately cover these cases. We're simply helping by placing that manpower where it is sorely needed, along the I-86 corridor," FBI Agent Rylie Wolf said.*

He scowled. He couldn't even take credit for the idea of developing the field office. That order had come directly from Washington. When the other Unit Chiefs had heard about it, they'd all rolled their eyes. "No man's land," they'd called it. "The assignment from hell."

And he could think of no place better for the agent from hell.

He'd wanted her gone. But his father had insisted she stay on. Firing would be too messy, he'd said. So, without much thought, he'd done the next best thing. He'd volunteered her for the I-86 assignment. An easy way to wrap up his problems with a bow and send them off, never to be seen again.

Now, he was seriously regretting it. Here, he could keep his thumb on her. Out in the Midwest, she had free reign to use her own reckless judgement and make things happen. And clearly, she was doing just that, unfettered by any rules like some wild west cowgirl. He'd thought that eventually, she'd become a victim of her own recklessness, but apparently not. Apparently, she was thriving.

And there was nothing that made a supervisor look worse than the agent he'd written off as a "problem," time and time again, making a one-eighty and being a hero in another unit.

"Rich!" he screamed again.

One of the agents who reported to him in the unit, Cooper Rich, was a solid guy. He did what he was told. He'd also been in pretty thick with Rylie Wolf. If anyone knew the dirt on her, Rich would.

Rich appeared in his doorway, leaning casually against the jamb. "Sorry, you called me? I was just working on the Arnoldson case you told me--"

"I don't care about that," he said with a wave of his hand. "I want to know about this."

He pointed to the computer screen in front of him. Rich, a good enough guy but a bit of a follower who'd had it easy in life on account of his good looks, came around the desk, hands thrust into the pockets of his slacks, and leaned in to read.

"Oh, yeah, another article on Rylie," he said with a smile. "I saw that one. She's killing it out there, huh?"

He let out a low, guttural growl. "Yeah. What do you know about it?"

He shrugged. "What do you mean?"

"I mean, you two were close. Have you talked to her since?"

"Sure have," he said with a smile. "Not much. She's obviously pretty busy out there. Kicking butt and taking names, as you can see. But she said she liked it. A lot more than she thought she would. She said it's certainly better than—"

He paused, allowing Bill to fill in the blanks. *Certainly better than here.*

Rich finished with, "Well, you know."

Bill nodded, thinking. Whoever Wolf's chief was out there probably hadn't noticed yet how unorthodox her practices could be. Maybe he should put a bug in her boss's ear, as a public service, to keep an eye on her. "Who's her supervising officer out there? Do you know?"

He shrugged. "She never said. Sure you can look that up."

"Does she have a partner? Is she working alone?"

Again, he shrugged, and raised an eyebrow. "Uh, Matthews, pardon me for asking, but why are you so concerned? She's none of your business anymore. Right?"

95

He pulled his lips into a tight scowl. She wasn't his business anymore, but that was only half of it. He'd wanted to bury her. Now, with her star shooting off into the stratosphere with all these high-profile cases, he could just see it. Rylie Wolf, passing him on the corporate ladder, becoming his boss. Screwing him in the process, the way he'd hoped to screw her.

Like hell. He'd die before he saw that happen.

"Just curious," he said lightly, motioning him away from his desk. "I always like to know how my former associates are getting on in the world. I want to know that they're happy and doing well. Because I care."

He smiled.

Cooper Rich smiled back. "You didn't need confirmation from me, did you? She *is* doing well, as you can see from the newspapers. Despite you sending her on what you thought would be the assignment from hell."

Bill Matthews gritted his teeth and pointed to the door. "Out. I expect to have data on that Arnoldson case by close of business."

Rich's smile widened. "I'm on it," he said, and headed for his desk.

Matthews leaned his head back and stared at the ceiling. Rylie Wolf may have been the FBI's shooting star, but it wouldn't last forever. Eventually, that star would fall.

Now, more than ever, he was determined to see it happen, even if he had to pull it out of the sky himself.

CHAPTER NINETEEN

Rylie sat on the porch of a cabin adjacent to the one Airlia had been murdered in, looking around as Michael peppered their latest possible witness, a harried forty-something father, with questions.

The more interviews that went on, the more she felt like she could answer the questions herself, and the less she spoke. Now, she was almost completely withdrawn, scanning the area, wondering how many more of these cabins they had to visit.

A couple of kids played in front of them, snapping their towels at each other and shrieking. The shrill sound of their cries almost split Rylie's skull.

This was wrong. If time was of the essence and the precious seconds were ticking down until the next crime was committed . . . then this was a waste of it.

Michael nudged her, which brought her back to the task at hand. "You have anything else to ask?"

Truthfully, she wasn't sure what he'd already asked. But the answers were always the same. *Did you see anything? No. Did you hear anything? No. Anything seem suspicious last night? Not that I can remember.*

She shook her head.

A mother came out of the cabin, wearing a white caftan and flip flops. "How much longer is this going to take?" she snapped. "The kids want to get to the indoor pool and they're getting restless."

The father nodded. "Yes . . . are we done here?"

Michael stood up. "Of course. We won't keep you. Thank you for your time."

He sighed and looked at the map of the complex as they stepped off the porch. "Well, that only leaves fifty more—"

"Let's stop," Rylie mumbled.

He pointed his pen at the map. "But—"

"We're getting nowhere. We've conducted interview after interview and no one saw anything. I think we're wasting time that can be better spent elsewhere."

He'd stepped off in the direction of the next cabin, but now, he stopped. "And where do you want to look?"

"I think we should go back to that motor lodge."

He tilted his head. "Did Beeker find something tying the new victim to that place?"

"No. In fact, he sent me the route and she wasn't anywhere near that place. But two of them, Bobette Langdon and Neez Ramirez, did stop there. And I can't help thinking that there's something about that place that—"

"Only two of them stopped there. The same number of people who stopped at the Blinking Star. Unless Airlia stopped at the Blinking S—"

"No, she didn't."

"All right, so half of them stopped there. That's fifty percent, an F, in my book. Why would you want to—"

"I guess I just have a feeling. I think we should talk to Henny's son, like we were planning to."

"That's great. And we will. But right now, we're here, and the killer chose this place for a reason. I just got a text from Officer Black that there's a hiking trail out back and a hole in the gate. The killer could've come in that way. I think we need to check it out, then keep our focus here, because—"

"I don't think so. I think—"

"Wolf. You said we should stick with the most recent victim. Well, here she is. This is where we're going to find the killer. Not in the past."

He started to stalk away, toward the perimeter fence. She watched him go, then grabbed her phone and texted Beeker: *Give me all the details you have about the Super Mo-Tel near Columbus-Laurel Montana.*

He responded a moment later: *With pleasure. And you're welcome.*

She gritted her teeth. She always seemed to forget that part. Reluctantly, she typed in a quick *Thank you* and rushed to join her partner.

When she reached him, he and a number of officers were standing by a large gap in the fence. They were staring at a number of footprints in the dirt, of all different types—men's boots, kids' Converse, a small, narrow footprint that belonged either to a child or a woman with small feet. There were dozens of them, all mixed together.

She gazed at it, wondering why all of them were so transfixed. "What does this tell us?" she announced. "Nothing, except that a lot of

98

people used this opening to reach the hiking trail, rather than go all the way around to the front of the complex."

Michael gave her a weary look, but Officer Black nodded. "She's right."

Michael said, "We should go out to the trail and see where it leads, if there are any other clues out there."

"I'll tell you where it leads," she muttered. "To a dead end."

Michael pressed his lips together but said nothing.

She knew he was frustrated with her, but she felt just the same. This was a total waste of time, and every second that ticked by only made her more annoyed. The motel was two hours away. If they were going to make it back there, they'd have to leave soon.

One by one, they all ducked their heads to go through the hole. The trail was a narrow, dirt path that led downhill, through the woods. They followed it for a few moments in silence, scanning the area for any clues. But the path was well-traveled, with many footprints and signs of human life, pieces of discarded trash. There was nothing to say any of this had come from the killer.

Waste of time, Rylie thought to herself.

When they went around the bend, the path stretched into the distance, nothing but trees ahead. "Officer Black," Michael said, stopping. "You have a map of this trail? Does it cross any roads or anything?"

Black looked at the map and shook his head. "Goes out to the canyon. About twenty miles. The only road it crosses is ten miles out."

Rylie rolled her eyes. "There's no way he traveled ten miles in the darkness and ten miles back in order to kill her. He must've come in from the front, and no one saw him."

Michael let out a frustrated grunt. "Yeah." He called to the other officers. "This is a waste. Let's head back."

Well, at least he's finally seeing it my way, she thought. "So you agree? We can go back to the motel now?"

"I didn't say that," he mumbled, picking up the pace.

"Then, what?"

He stopped short and pointed at the map of the complex in his hands. He had a list of the places they'd already done questioning, half of them crossed out. "I think we need to stick with the questioning here."

"But it's bull," she snapped, hands on her hips. "Why? So you can hear, *I didn't see anything* another four-hundred times?"

They stood there, in the middle of the trail, staring one another down. The other officers walked past them and when they were far enough away that they wouldn't hear him, he said, "Look. Officer Black said that Airlia Birnbaum's boyfriend, Brock Hamilton, from Boston, is on the way. I think we should stay here and wait until—"

"Are you kidding me? He's coming from Boston? It'll take him forever to—"

"He's some attorney there, with connections. His firm is letting him use their private plane, and he's flying directly into Sheridan County airport, so they're expecting him within the next few hours. When we're done with questioning the guests of the resort, then we can ask him—"

"And I told you, that's a waste of time, too. What is he going to tell us? He was in Boston. She was in Montana."

"Black said Hamilton spoke to her from the road the night before she was murdered. He might be able to shed some light on where she was, what she was up to."

"What she was *up to* was trying to get back east to be with him. We know that. And I know where she was," she muttered, holding up her phone. "Her phone records indicate she spent the night prior in a town called Reed Point."

"Which is nowhere near the motel you want to go to," he pointed out.

"Yes, but maybe we should check that out, too. The killer obviously followed her from someplace up there. So where did he come from? *Up there.* Staying down here is just a distraction. It's designed to keep us out of the way."

He eyed her for a long time, before sighing. "You know what? I'm done arguing this with you. You say this is wasting time? You're wasting time, arguing it with me. We could've made some real headway by now if you'd just shut up and let me—"

"Shut up?" She stared at him in indignation. "You want me to just shut up? Who the hell do you think you are?"

He blinked, and something in his face told her he didn't want to get into this with her. But he had. And now, they were going to have it out. "I'm the guy who's following protocol and finishing this investigation. And if you knew what was good for you, you'd do so, too."

She snorted. "I know what's good for me. And you know what? I don't care. I do what's good for the investigation. Because I want to solve these crimes. That's all that matters to me."

100

His eyes narrowed. He shook his head. "And that's exactly why you're going to get yourself killed one day. You take things too personally. That thing with your sister? No one will touch it, and they have good reason for that. It's over. Done. So cold it's in a block of ice. But you're going to kill yourself trying to find the answers there. And I might be your partner, but I have a bit of common sense left. And I'm not going to be dragged down into it with you. Hell no."

She stared at him, seething. *This* was why she'd never gotten along with a partner. *This* was why she'd never told anyone about Maren. Because they all thought she was crazy. So what if she didn't do everything by the book? She made things happen. But they all thought she was going to go off half-cocked and get them killed. Bill Matthews, Jerry Matthews, Cooper Rich . . . None of them had the balls to stand up for her.

And now, add Michael Brisbane to the list. She'd thought he was different. She'd thought he'd had little bit of cowboy in him, that he might thumb his nose at the powers that be and help her.

But she was wrong.

She didn't think too much on her next move. In fact, she didn't think at all. Without warning, she dove forward, reached into the pocket of his blazer, and grabbed the keys to his truck.

He reached for her, but she squirmed out of his grasp and took off running.

"I'll bring it back when I'm done!" she shouted over her shoulder as she ran, wildly, up the path and into the complex. She heard him running after her, shouting her name, but she didn't stop running until she'd gotten to his truck.

Now, the investigation could proceed. On her terms.

CHAPTER TWENTY

Michael Brisbane trudged to the next cabin and knocked on the door. According to his list, this cabin was occupied by an older couple, Mr. & Mrs. Seth Fredrick. It was the last cabin on his list of fifty, and he'd be happy to be done with it.

He hated to admit it, but Rylie—the rotten truck-stealer—had been right. It had been a waste of time. He only hoped that when Brock Hamilton arrived, he'd be of more help.

The door opened, and a woman who was probably no more than twenty-five looked out. She had platinum curls, falling in her face, a victim of bedhead. And she was wearing nothing more than a sheet, wrapped around her center.

She giggled. "Hi?"

"Uh, hello . . . Mrs. Frederick?"

She giggled some more. "Sure . . . if you want to call me that." She fluffed her hair. "Who are you? You don't look like room service."

"I'm from the FBI, actually," he said, flipping his credentials. "My name is—"

"Meem, who is it?" a gravelly old voice called.

Her eyes were focused on his badge. "Oh, Sethy, it's a man from the FBI. You haven't been a bad boy, have you?"

An old man came to the door, wearing nothing but boxers. His chest was bird-like and covered with the same wiry white hair that was on his head. His face was ruddy and his nose, bulbous. He eyed Michael from head to toe. "I'm Seth Frederick. What do you want?"

"It's nothing you did, sir. There was a murder in the complex last night, and we're just asking routine questions of all the guests."

"Oooh! We're suspects!" Meem giggled. "How thrilling. Are you going to pat me down?"

"You're not suspects," Brisbane said stiffly, putting away his credentials. "I just had a few questions as to whether or not you heard or saw anything last night."

The old man squeezed the young girl's side. "I saw my beautiful bride's face, as I made love to her," he said as she erupted in more flattered giggles. "Tell me, man. If you could look at this woman for any length of time you chose, why would you want to look anywhere else?"

"Aw, you're so sweet," she gushed, kissing the top of his head. "But it's true. He and I got here last night and we've been dead to the rest of the world since. It's our honeymoon! So I don't think we can help you."

"Yeah. You know what? Forget it," he said, scratching off the rest of his questions and backing away. "Those are all the questions I have for you today. I appreciate your help. Enjoy the rest of your honeymoon."

He stepped from the porch, sighing as the door slammed behind him.

Now, he had nothing to do but to wait until Brock Hamilton arrived.

He meandered about, trying to think of who else he could question or what else he could do. They'd already searched the victim's cabin and car, finding very little of interest. They'd checked the trail out back, and that had brought in even less. They'd spoken to the maintenance staff and the front desk clerk, but no one could recall any other vehicles or persons in the vicinity of the cabin. They'd interviewed most of the three-hundred guests. It'd been a long, exhaustive process . . . and, just as Rylie had said, it'd been completely worthless. They hadn't gotten a single clue as to who this killer was.

Not to mention that he was now stranded here, in the middle of Montana, with no way to get to her. *Thanks, Rylie Wolf. Thanks a lot,* he thought bitterly. *You're a real great partner.*

Maybe it was his own fault. He hadn't been the best of partners, either. Maybe he should've opened up more to her, when she'd gone and told him about her past. She had a reason to be bitter with him. He'd been a total ass to her, basically telling her he didn't care.

But he did. More than she knew. He just . . . didn't want to open that up with her. To cross that line. He'd talk about anything with her, but that. He had that wall up for a reason. No crossing allowed, ever. The more he went down that path with her, the more vulnerable it made both of them.

And Rylie was putting them in danger. She didn't know the meaning of the word compromise. That wasn't what partners did. They communicated. Talked things out. Agreed together. They didn't just barrel forward with their own ideas.

And the thing was, he would've gone along with her. If she'd just held her damn horses and waited a little while, until they'd finished up here. How hard was that?

No . . . no, he was in the right here.

It must've been his past pulling at him, though, because it didn't stop him from feeling guilty. Just as guilty as he had when he found out
. . .

No . . . don't think about it. That's what he usually did. That's why he was able to keep that smile on his face. When those dark thoughts threatened to intrude, he shut them down before they could take root and poison his mind.

He pulled out his phone and placed another call to her, his tenth in the two hours since she'd left. It went right to voicemail.

This time, he left her a voicemail. "Look. I'm not mad. If you come back and bring my truck, we can work this out and figure out a compromise. But we're partners for a reason, and Kit would want us to work together, Wolf. We're supposed to have each other's back. Call me back."

He ended the call and sighed. She was too stubborn. She wouldn't.

And who knew what kind of danger she might put herself in?

He scanned the area around him. The crowds had thinned out, since word got around about the murder, but there were still a few hardy souls, sticking around, riding the horseback trails and heading toward the pool facilities.

He wished he could be as lighthearted. But there was a killer out there, and he needed answers.

And so naturally, his thoughts turned to what they usually turned to, at a time like this.

Food.

The smell from the restaurant at the front of the complex was one of French fries and hamburgers, exactly what his stomach was crying out for. It was nothing special, but it was a little nicer than the Blinking Star. Thankfully, his stomach had fully recuperated from that little adventure.

He started to climb the steps, wondering if they could make him a vanilla shake to dip his fries in, when he heard the sound of tires crunching on gravel behind him and saw a dark stretch limo pull through the gates.

He didn't need to guess who that was. It didn't exactly blend with the rest of the clientele.

104

He reversed direction and headed toward the limo, just as the driver stepped out and opened the back door. A sea of dark, windblown hair appeared, and a tanned, handsome face wearing dark, Top Gun shades. The man was wearing a suit, and he lowered his shades slightly over his nose and scanned the area in disgust. "Ivan, see if you can call the office and cancel the Friday—"

"Brock Hamilton?" Michael Brisbane started, moving forward to introduce himself before the driver could even close the door.

It was only at that moment that he realized the man was on a hands-free call, a Bluetooth in his ear. He held up a finger and said, "Yes. Cancel. Good."

He pulled the earpiece out and stared at Michael.

Michael started again. "Brock Hamilton?"

"That's right," he murmured, and it was only then that Michael heard a slight British accent. "What is this place? Some kind of . . . what do they call it? A dude ranch?"

"Yeah, it's a resort," Michael said. "I'm sorry about your loss. I'm sure it must've been a terrible shock for you."

"Ah, well, you know. Stiff upper lip and all. That's the British way," he said shortly, brushing a bit of imaginary dust from his impeccable suit jacket.

"You are from the UK?"

"Born, yes. I've been living in Boston. That's where I came from. Anyhow, I had to see first-hand how something like this could've possibly happened. Clearly this place isn't very well guarded." He lifted his nose into the air and sniffed, almost as if he was smelling the lawsuit. "Where was security when all of this was transpiring?"

"The complex doesn't have security, unfortunately. It's really not necessary in a place like this," he explained, then realized he hadn't introduced himself. "I'm—"

"You're not security?" Brock asked, running a suspicious eye over him.

"No, I'm Michael Brisbane, of the FBI." He showed his credentials.

Brock read them with disinterest. "The FBI. All right. Good. I'm glad the federal authorities are involved. Then you should be able to tell me who did this to Airlia, and why?"

"We're looking into it. We—"

"Well, look harder. You know, Airlia is part of the Boston Birnbaums. Her father passed away last year, but I can tell you that he'll be rolling over in his grave if this case goes unsolved. Do you

105

understand? Her mother's frail, and this will hit her hard. I'm looking out for her family, and there are many people—powerful people—who will have your head if the person who did this to her isn't found."

Michael thought of the hundreds of people he'd just interviewed and gritted his teeth. "We're doing everything we possibly can."

"Do. More," he said with a scowl. "I want to see the suite she rented. Take me there. Now."

After getting stranded by his partner, being treated like Brock Hamilton's personal slave wasn't exactly sitting well with Michael Brisbane. Clenching his fists at his sides to keep from exploding, he walked the man to the back of the complex. The attorney's face took on a more and more horrified expression, the deeper they went, past rag-tag kids in flip flops, piles of manure from the horses, and broken-down supply sheds. When they stopped in front of the cabin, he shook his head.

"Here? She couldn't have stayed here."

Brisbane shrugged. "She did. I'm sorry to say that her body was found there."

He shook his head. "I don't believe it. I simply don't believe it." Hands on his hips, he went to the door, ducking under the yellow crime scene tape.

"You probably shouldn't disturb that—" Michael stopped when it became clear the man was going to proceed, no matter what he said. He watched the man peer inside the room and turn back in disgust.

"Why?" He went to her car and kicked the tire with his shiny black shoe. "It was this damn foolish car of hers. She loved it. I told her that I could put her on a flight, first class, and we could be together. But she insisted on this foolish trip. She had to bring her car—her baby—out with her, and she wanted to 'see the country' before she came back. Stupid idea. But I couldn't convince her. She was too headstrong. She could've at least picked a place nicer than this. I had the names of plenty of nice establishments, but she wanted an adventure. Well, she got one."

"I see," Michael said, leaning against the porch rail as the man paced back and forth. "When was the last time you spoke to her?"

"Night before last," he said, shaking his head. "She was staying at some dive motel somewhere in who-knows-where. We argued."

"About what?"

"About her safety, of course. I was worried she was going to do something stupid. She usually did. She was very forgetful, very

106

reckless. She'd stopped somewhere to get something to eat and left her phone there. When she called me, it was from the hotel phone. I'd told her she needed to call that place straight away and see if they had it." He shook his head. "She was always doing things like that. I don't know if she ever found it."

"She did. It was found in her room," he said.

"Ah, well. This must've happened before nine because we have a strict schedule. She must call me to check in at nine," he explained. "I work until eight and I'm not home until then. If she doesn't call me at nine, then I know to be worried. And I was very worried last night. As soon as I got the call from the police, I knew . . ."

"Yes, I'm sure," Michael said. "It must've been very distressing for you."

He nodded. "Not to mention inconvenient. I'm about to try the biggest case of my career in a few days."

Too bad she didn't coordinate her schedule with yours better, he thought, staring at the man. "When you last spoke to her, did she mention anything about anyone strange she met, while traveling?"

"No. But that was Airlia. Everyone was always staring at her, but she was oblivious. Did you see a picture of her? She's stunning." He pressed his lips together. "*Was* stunning. We were planning to get married this summer, when I finished with this case. Well, she kept saying she didn't want to, she was the independent type, but I'd just about worn her down. Having a wife . . . especially one from a good family like Airlia, it conveys a certain amount of prestige, stability, to my clients. You understand."

"Of course."

"But the problem was that Airlia never seemed to understand that. She was perfectly happy eating at a fast-food restaurant or staying at a place like this." He looked around, his lips pursed in distaste. "The last place she called me from, she said half the motel had burned down in a fire. It probably wasn't even up to code. She had no idea what kind of danger—"

"Burned down in a fire?" he repeated the words, something tickling at the back of his brain. The Super Mo-Tel Montana. "Did she say the name of it?"

Brock shook his head.

"Did she say where it was?"

He shook his head again. "Somewhere on the interstate, I assume. She said it was the only place for miles, so she was forced to stay there."

His blood went cold. "That's where she called you from . . . and she didn't have her phone?"

"Right." Brock eyed him curiously. "I just told you that. She'd left it somewhere when she stopped to eat."

Suddenly, the pieces clicked into place. Airlia Birnbaum *had* been at the Super Mo-Tel Montana, but of course they'd had no record of it because they'd been tracking the victims by their cell phones. And she hadn't brought her cell phone with her that night.

That meant that at least three out of the four victims had been at the motel that Rylie was suspicious of.

And those were good enough odds for him.

He needed to go after Rylie. He'd hop in his truck and head out . . .

No. He couldn't do that. She had his truck.

"Hey, listen," he said to Brock, motioning to the police officers. "I just thought of something I need to take care of."

Officer Black came over. "Brock Hamilton?"

"Yeah," Michael Brisbane said, making the introductions. Then he took the officer aside. "Look, I just got a hot lead on the case up north, but my partner has my vehicle. Can I borrow one of yours and bring it back in a few hours?"

He nodded and handed him the keys. "Sure. It's parked at the office. We'll still be here, finishing up. Otherwise you can drop it at headquarters."

"Great. Will do."

He began to back up, but then the officer said, "What kind of hot lead? Related to this case?"

"Yeah. It's a bit of an emergency," he said, grabbing his phone. He raced back to the front of the complex and jumped in the car, pulling out in a hurry. As he did, he dialed Rylie, but she let the phone go to voicemail. She was probably still pissed at him.

But now he had to wonder if he would make it there in time to save her from whatever danger lurked at that seedy motel.

CHAPTER TWENTY ONE

Rylie played with the dial of the radio, trying to find something other than country. Michael Brisbane was a clear country boy, every preset button on it was tuned to that kind of music. Finally, she found a staticky channel that played heavy metal, with a driving beat and shouting rather than singing. It suited her mood.

As she approached the Super Mo-Tel Montana, her phone rang. It was Michael, probably wanting her to come back. He'd probably feed her the same sad lines about how partners were supposed to stay together, have each other's backs, blah blah blah.

No, no, no, Bris, sorry, she thought to herself. *I'm not going to let you guilt trip me into turning around.*

Besides, she'd told him, when they first started working together, that she was used to working on her own. Running the show herself. If he wanted them to stay together, it was simple—he just had to agree to do what she told him to do.

She did feel guilty about taking his truck, though. He'd said more than once that it was his baby, and she understood why. It was only a couple months old and ran like a dream. It blew her own pick-up out of the water.

The song ended, and she glanced at her phone. He'd left her a voicemail.

Nope. Not listening, she thought, taking her phone in her hand and deleting it unread. As she was doing that, her phone began to ring with a call from Beeker.

That one, she was eager to answer. She brought the phone to her ear. "Beeker? You find anything?"

"And hello to you," he grumbled.

Funny how no matter how many times she spoke to him, she never learned. "Sorry. Hello."

"Yeah, anyway, about that motel. I didn't find much. There was a fire there a few years back and from what I heard, they got the insurance money."

She nodded. "If they did, they sure didn't use the money to fix the place up."

"But there's something else. It's a decade old case, though. So it probably has no bearing on what you're looking into, but I thought I should mention it."

Her stomach fluttered. "What's that?"

"Well . . . it was the murder of a woman who stayed there. Never solved. She was a Jane Doe. No one ever identified her. It was assumed she was a prostitute, whose john refused to pay, murdered her, and fled. Witnesses heard a lot of screaming before it happened. But you know those kinds of cases—with no one pushing for the killer to be found, it slipped between the cracks."

"Yeah. That's sad," she said, thinking. Prostitute murders at seedy hotels happened all the time. She'd run into at least a dozen cold cases like that, since she started with the FBI. So it was only fitting that a dive like the Super Mo-Tel had its own prostitute murder story. It likely didn't have anything to do with the case at hand. "Nothing else?"

"They had a few health violations over the years, a couple domestic violence situations. One report of a robbery. But these all happened years ago. Other than that, the Super Mo-Tel is clean."

She snorted. "It's not that clean. Bris and I stayed there. It smelled like feet and garbage. And not Brisbane's feet, either."

He chuckled, but suddenly became serious. "Wait . . . you stayed in a room together?"

She ignored that question. She was coming up to the exit for the motel anyway, and had to plan her next steps. "Just send me over the report, okay?"

"You got it. Bye!" he said, ending the call.

She put on her blinker and took her foot off the gas as she approached the ramp and the motel came into view. In daylight, it looked a lot less ominous than before. She'd had a strange sense of foreboding and intuition when she'd thought about the place earlier, but now, it was gone.

She bit on her lip. Maybe she was just jumping to wild conclusions out of desperation. Maybe she had been a little rash, stealing Brisbane's car and heading out on her own. He probably had every reason to hate her.

Her phone rang again. It was Bris. Again.

This time, she answered. "Look, I know you're upset that I took your truck. And maybe I reacted rashly, but you have to understand—"

110

"You might be right, Wolf."

The words stopped her in her tracks. They were the last words she was expecting. "What?"

"I just spoke to Brock Hamilton. Airlia Birnbaum's boyfriend from Boston. He told me that she stayed at a hotel fitting the description of the Super Mo-Tel."

"Really? Are you sure? Because her phone records—"

"I'm ninety-nine percent positive. Supposedly, she stopped somewhere and left her phone there by accident, and had to go back the following morning and get it."

"Oh," Rylie whispered, pulling into the parking lot of the place. She was already starting to get that foreboding feeling back. "I'm here now. I'll ask—"

"I'm on my way. I should be there in a couple hours."

"On your way? But how—"

"Officer Black lent me his patrol car."

She let out an uneasy breath as she navigated into the parking lot. It was empty again, just as it'd been the first time they arrived there. "I am not waiting for you that long."

"I didn't expect you would." There was a pause. "Just call me if you find anything out."

"I will."

She stepped out of the car and hurried into the office. The smell of cigar smoke was heavy in the small room. Henny was sitting on the lumpy, flowered sofa, paging through the same magazine her son had been reading the night before. She had her feet clad in red cowboy boots, up on the coffee table, and was chewing on the cigar. She didn't look up.

"Hello," Rylie said, as loudly as she could. "Henny?"

The woman turned and squinted at her. "Eh? Oh, it's you. Well, what do you know. We don't get many return visitors. You come to stay this time?"

She was struggling to get out of her chair, but Rylie quickly said, "No, I stayed last night, thank you. Your son checked me in. But this time, I don't want a room. I just have a few more questions for you."

The lady sat back and puffed on her cigar. "Questions? Oh, right. You're that CIA woman."

"FBI. Right."

She motioned with a wrinkled hand for Rylie to get on with it.

111

Rylie pulled up the photograph of Nick Costas. "I was wondering if you'd seen this guy, at all? His name is Nick Costas. He stayed here, maybe a week ago."

She squinted. "I can't tell. I can barely see anything."

"You have credit card statements? Something that he might've used to show that he was here and paid?"

The woman let out a loud harrumph. "Are you kidding? I do, somewhere. But my son takes care of all that. I don't know where they are. I don't know much about that newfangled credit card stuff."

Rylie walked to the counter. "So do you keep a record at all of who has stayed with you?"

She motioned to the counter at the same time Rylie noticed the old, leatherbound ledger, underneath a pile of papers. "I have people sign that guestbook."

Rylie frowned. "We didn't sign a guestbook when we—"

"That's because my Charlie always forgets to tell people to do it. But if you take a room with me, you sign the book."

Rylie reached over and grabbed it, before realizing she should probably ask permission. "May I?"

"Feel free," Henny said, blowing out a thick cloud of smoke. "Anything for the CIA."

"Thanks," she said, pulling it out from under the pile of paperwork and cracking it open.

She scanned the list of signatures and dates. They hadn't had many guests recently; on a single page, the date went back several months. Using her finger to scan the list, she saw it, about halfway down the page. *Nicholas Costas.*

There it was. She gave herself a mental pat on the back and scanned the rest of the page, looking for more. No Bobette Langdon, though Rylie was pretty sure she'd wanted to make other arrangements. No Airlia Birnbaum, but Michael had confirmed she was there. She almost missed it, but then she caught it, a few lines from down from Nick's name: *Ebenezer Ramirez.*

So they'd all stayed at this motel before their deaths.

She felt like she'd climbed a mountain. The hardest part was behind them. But still, there was more to uncover. What did it mean? What did this place have to do with their deaths?

She turned to the old woman. "I need to speak to your son. You said his name was Charlie?"

She snorted. "Charlie? Good luck. He works a bunch of other jobs. He's never home. I don't know where he is right now."

Rylie sighed. "All right. Then do you have any other employees who work here? Housekeeping? Maintenance?"

"I don't have much help. Don't have the cashflow to have that luxury, darlin'. Charlie helps out with what I need done. He's my right hand. But other than that, I'm on my own."

"Charlie does everything for you? Washing the towels, cleaning the rooms?"

She shrugged. "Just about. I rely on the kindness of others to help me out."

"So you don't have any employees at all?"

The old lady frowned. "Well, I got Emily. She's a maid. She does the things I can't do. But she's only here a couple hours a day. I don't think of her as an actual employee, though. More like a friend."

"All right, great. Can I talk to her?"

Henny shrugged. "Yeah. Go right ahead. She's probably cleaning the room next door. People there had a party and trashed it last night."

Rylie raised an eyebrow in surprise. Was she really so tired last night that she'd missed a rowdy party? Had Michael noticed that? "Okay, great. And do you know when Charlie will be in again?"

She stubbed her cigar out in the ashtray on the coffee table. "Now, let me see. He stops by, throughout the day, darlin'. He's barely ever home at his trailer up in Laurel, or else I'd tell you to stop there. Your best bet is to catch him here. If he comes in, I'll tell him you're looking for him and ask him to wait, if you're planning to stay close by. Okay?"

"Great. Thanks. I will. Let me give you my number, and you can call me when he comes in, okay?" She scribbled it down in extra-big print for the woman to read, and went to the door to make her exit.

"He ain't in any trouble, is he?" Henny called after her, staring at the paper.

"No. No trouble. Just have some routine questions, like I asked of you."

"Oh. All right. Charlie's a good boy, so I didn't think so. Doesn't bring my grandbabies around nearly enough, but I guess there's worse things one can do, right?" She smiled. "Well, I hope whatever you're looking for, you find it, dear. I don't want any trouble around here. We try to run a respectable, family business."

113

Something clicked in Rylie's head. "Oh. That reminds me of another thing I wanted to ask you. This business has been in your family a long time, right?"

Henny chuckled. "Oh, years and years. My grandparents ran it when I was a little girl. Back then, that gas station across the street was a one-room schoolhouse. There were two of us in my graduating class. Can you believe that?"

Rylie smiled. "No. That's interesting. Hey, tell me more about the woman who was murdered in one of these rooms?"

The old woman's smile fell, and she shuddered slightly. "Poor woman. No one knew who she was. She had her throat slit. I saw her myself. Lying, face-down, naked on the bed, the sheets drenched in blood. Not one of my better days on this earth. I will never forget that, as long as I live."

"It's true they never caught who did it?"

She nodded. "I saw the man she was with. I gave him the key. I knew when I looked into his eyes that there was something wrong with him. His eyes were dark. Cold. Like two stones. I shudder to think of it. I gave the police the description, but it did no good. Never caught the beast."

She seemed to draw into herself, remembering that day, because she trembled visibly.

"Thank you," Rylie said, and headed out the door to find the maid, trying to shake off the haunting image of a man with cold, dark, dead eyes.

CHAPTER TWENTY TWO

Rylie texted Michael as soon as she stepped outside, a little spring in her step as she basked in the victory.

Bingo. It's like I thought. Nick Costas did stay here, too.

She wouldn't gloat, though, the next time she saw him. She didn't need to. He'd have to see that she was clearly in the right—that sometimes, her flashes of intuition, though inexplicable and out of nowhere, had merit. That's why she simply couldn't come to a compromise with him. Next time, she could bring this instance up, and maybe he wouldn't argue with her so much.

But even better than that, they were making progress. They had the X that marked the spot where they needed to dig. Now they just had to do the work and find what they'd come for.

He didn't respond, probably because he was still making his way toward her. She knew he was still at least an hour away, so she went to the first room next to the office, number one, past a small alley with the ice maker and vending machine. The door was slightly open.

She peeked in. "Hello?"

Her eyes adjusted to the light and focused on a portly woman with a dark pixie haircut, standing on one of the beds in her stocking feet. She was scrubbing something that looked like spray paint off the wall, and not having much luck.

"What?" the woman growled, not looking back.

Rylie took a couple steps in and looked around in horror. Someone had drawn a bunch of Satanic symbols and 666 all over the wallpaper and cheap paintings. It looked like spray paint. "Oh, my gosh," she said, nearly tripping over a pile of beer cans in the doorway.

"Yeah, lovely, isn't it?" the woman grouched, shaking out her hand and then trying again. "And I bet you Charlie let them pay cash, so they're gone with the wind. They won't be able to charge them for damages."

"Do you know who they were?"

115

"No clue. Just some teenagers, probably. Having fun. I don't know, when I was a teen, having fun was going to dances and the movies. Not pulling this crap. Look at what they did!"

When she jumped off the bed, rather ungracefully, and looked around, Rylie realized she had a long, punk-inspired shock of hair falling in her face, dyed bright lime green.

"There's no saving this. I guess I'm going to have to tell Henny she needs to get this place a whole new paint job. She's not going to be happy. She doesn't have the cash as it is. But it's Charlie's fault for letting them stay without getting any info on them." She threw the wet rag down and wiped her hands on the back of her jeans, then blew the shock of hair out of her eyes. "And who are you?"

Rylie opened her wallet and flashed her badge. "I'm Rylie Wolf with the FBI. I'm investigating a string of murders, trying to see what the victims have in common. And it turns out, they all stayed at this motel."

She put her hands on her fleshy hips. "Seriously? Is it too much to hope that one of the victims was the person who did this?"

"Uh . . ." The joke—was it a joke?— took Rylie by surprise. She'd expected shock, but this woman was all-too-nonchalant about the whole thing. Clearly, Emily wasn't one to be surprised by much. From Rylie's experience, people like that had usually had a rough life.

The woman smirked. "Sorry. I've just spent three hours, scrubbing my elbow off, and I've gotten zero result. So how many victims are we talking about? You're sure they stayed here? Recently? Is this like a serial killing?"

"Possibly. And yes, recently. That it's a serial killing is something we're considering."

"They all women?"

"No, actually not. It doesn't seem like the killer picked a physical type."

She sat on the edge of the bed and slipped into her white, scuffed sneakers. "That's crazy. And in our own little town. I did hear on the news about a couple murders in the area. But I never realized that they all stayed here. Not that I'd have remembered them. I usually arrive to work after the guests have checked out." She shook her head, pushing the shock of green hair out of her eyes. "Otherwise I'd have run those hooligans out the second I heard a sound. But poor Henny. She's such an innocent. Good-hearted lady. And people take advantage of her."

"Henny said that you work for her part-time?"

She nodded. "That's right. The pay's crap but I know it's all the old lady can afford. So I humor her. She lets me stop in when I finish the breakfast shift at Hardee's. It's too much for the old lady. I keep trying to gently convince her to close this place down, but she won't hear of it. The place has been in her family for ages."

"You're the only other person who works here, besides Charlie?"

"I'm the only one who works here regularly. But she has a sweet, little-old-lady thing going for her, and she uses it to her advantage. She can usually con people into feeling sorry for her and helping her out with things she and Charlie can't do, like fixing a leaky toilet or a broken light switch." She eyed the place. "She'll have to pour the charm on thick to one of them, to get this room painted and ready to rent out again, I bet. It's beyond what I can do, that's for sure."

Rylie walked deeper into the room, looking at the mess. Wet toilet paper had been strewn all over the place and it smelled thickly of urine and vomit. She winced. "Do you know any of the names of the maintenance people that help her, or where I could find them?"

She shook her head. "I don't even think Henny knows them very well. She just gets them to help, and pays them with some fresh-baked biscuits—she makes good biscuits, from scratch—and then sends them on their way." She chuckled. "Guess that's the way people did things, back in the day. Bartering for services. Helping neighbors out. I think there are a few regular ones . . . but like I said, I don't know them well and doubt Henny does, either."

"So you have no idea where any of these people are? They just show up out of nowhere?" Rylie couldn't help but find that hard to believe. "What if something's broken and needs to be fixed? Who does she call?"

"Whoever she can find. She's not above asking some of her guests for help, either. Anyone who stops by, really, she'll rope into changing lightbulbs or what have you. I'm surprised she didn't try to get you to do something for her." She started to shake her head again, but then her mouth dropped open. "Oh. There's Barney. I know him by name. I don't know why I forgot about him. Probably cause he's kind of quiet and skulks around a lot. I haven't seen him in a long time because he's usually here late at night."

"Barney? He's a maintenance man?" This sounded promising. He'd likely have access to the rooms.

"No. Just another hand. Usually minds the front desk or changes lightbulbs. That kind of thing. He's just a kid, though. I don't think he's more than nineteen. He lives out past the highway, near the old Sip 'n' Pump, the gas station and beer store that closed down a while back. His parents used to run it. But Charlie gets him to come in and mind the front desk, whenever he and Henny can't be there." She smiled. "He's a little stand-offish, quiet, if you know what I mean, but Henny says he's pretty reliable. They really need the money, since their business shut down a few years ago. Both of his parents are disabled and never leave the house. So Henny pays him under the table."

She winced.

"Whoops! You're a fed. I probably shouldn't have said that last part. Can I have that stricken from the record, or whatever you do? Can you keep it just between us?"

"Of course. None of this is on the record, anyway. It's not an official interview. So . . . this old gas station. That's where Barney lives? Where is it?"

"Yeah. He lives in the old farmhouse behind it. You really can't miss it, if you go under the underpass for the highway. Maybe a mile down the road, across from the old cottages. On the right."

She straightened. "You think he's at home, right now?"

Emily shrugged. "You can try it. I don't think he holds a steady job because he always seems to be available when Charlie needs him. He drives a blue Chevy Nova. Real old. Fixed it up himself."

"Thanks," she said, heading to the door. "I think I will. I appreciate your time."

"No problem. And please . . .," She reached out and grabbed Rylie's arm. Rylie turned to find Emily's eyes pleading with her. "Don't say anything about the under-the-table thing? Poor Henny's barely hanging on as it is, and Barney doesn't have the easiest time, looking after both his parents."

She smiled. "You have my word. I understand."

She went outside to the truck and looked around. No sign yet of Michael. Checking her phone, she sighed. If she had it right, he probably wouldn't show up for another hour.

Rylie climbed into the driver's seat and texted him: *Checking out a lead with someone named Barney, who helps sometimes at the front desk. Wait for me at Motel.*

That was good enough. She'd kept him apprised of what she was doing, which was a lot more than she'd done for her other partners. It was his own fault he hadn't come with her, when she told him she wanted to check the place out again.

118

She pulled out, onto the road that ran under the highway. She knew she should wait for her partner . . . but she felt like she was wasting time, sitting there, doing nothing. She'd just drive over, try to find the gas station, and see if the blue Chevy Nova was there. There was no harm in that . . . right?

CHAPTER TWENTY THREE

As Rylie drove, she was vaguely aware that this was the route that Bobette had driven, the night she was killed. According to the log she'd gotten from Beeker, Bobette had gone up and down the road, searching for something. Likely, a place to stay. When she'd learned that the Super Mo-Tel was the only place at the exit, she'd almost stayed there, but chickened out at the last moment.

Rylie couldn't blame her. But she also couldn't help thinking that merely stopping there had doomed her. She hadn't even rented a room. And yet someone must've seen her. Someone must've followed her across the street to the gas station parking lot.

She shuddered at the thought as a number of small, broken-down cabins came into view. Most had broken windows and many were missing shingles, and a few had no doors. One had collapsed altogether. A sign out front said: *LAUREL SPRINGS COZY COTTAGES – CLOSED FOR SEASON.*

Closed for season? She wondered what season that was. It looked like they were closed for good. Maybe Bobette had driven out this way, hoping to stay there, only to find out that it wasn't open.

The bright sun was falling lower in the sky, making it difficult to see the landscape to her right. But there, across the street, she noticed the broken shed and old-style gas pumps. There was a sign there, too, but it had faded from the elements to nothing but white. There was a small, two-story farmhouse, set back from the road. A sign in the front window, near the door, said, GAS STATION CLOSED NO TRESPASSING NO SOLICITING.

No wonder it had closed down. There wasn't much to get off the highway for, on this exit, but on this side of the highway, there was barely anything but long stretches of barren land. Not to mention that Randy's gas station, on the other side of the highway, while not super-modern, was in a little better condition. This gas station had probably gone out of business around the same time as the cottages.

She scanned the farmhouse. All the windows and doors were closed, the shades pulled tight. It looked abandoned, too.

But then she noticed, parked to the side of the house, among some trees, the blue Chevy Nova.

She pulled to the grassy side of the road and idled there, thinking. Okay, the smart thing to do would be to wait for Michael. What if this guy was a killer and pulled a gun on her? But then again, if she posed no threat, he'd have no reason to. Yes. All she had to do was go to the door and tell whoever answered that she was lost and looking for directions. That way, she could at least check his vibe.

Perfect.

Just as she was about to pull into the station's parking lot, the door suddenly opened. A tall, lanky man with tattoos up and down both arms came out. He was wearing thick boots, dark jeans, and a black tank top. He strutted over to his Chevy Nova, and slid inside.

Okay, there he is, she said to herself. *Barney, in the flesh. What's his vibe?*

He seemed a little . . . shifty. It wasn't just the tattoos, but way he walked, so full of confidence, like nothing could touch him. But was it a serial killer vibe?

She couldn't tell. She needed more to go on.

A few seconds later, the car roared to life. Tires squealed as he peeled out into the road, leaving a cloud of dust behind him.

Sorry, Michael, but the early bird gets the worm, and I am not waiting for you, she thought, shifting into drive and taking off after him.

He drove away from the highway, and she followed, a good distance behind. Emily had made him seem more like a kid, but he hadn't looked that way to her. He'd looked like a full-grown man. A tough one, who'd probably wouldn't be so nice to her if he knew she was following him.

Could he have killed all those people? Could he have given them their room keys, taken down their license plate numbers and followed them after they left, only to murder them wherever they stopped next? If so, why? Did he kill for the sheer pleasure of it, or was there something more? She stared ahead, blinking away the bright sunlight, trying to figure out what his game was, and what his next move would be.

After about a mile or so, he made a quick right turn onto a street called Sweeping Pine Road, and she followed. They wound up in a small village with a bunch of empty storefronts, a post office, an auto parts store and a single stoplight, swaying overhead in the fierce wind.

121

The light was red, so she wound up pulling right behind him. Trying not to be too obvious, she checked his reflection in his side-mirror. He had his window down, was wearing dark sunglasses and smoking a cigarette. He looked a little like a young Mick Jagger, with full lips and longish, oily dark hair.

The light turned green. He proceeded through it, then without using a blinker, turned onto a side road, into a residential area of small, fifties-style ranch houses with chain-link fences. She followed, wishing she wasn't so close. She noticed him, lifting his chin as if to glance in his rear-view mirror. He was going to notice her, sooner or later, if he hadn't already.

As she wondered whether she should pull down another street, he suddenly pulled to the curb. Stiffening, she continued on, deliberately not looking his way, though she could've sworn he had his eyes on her as she went past.

Her heart beating fast, she took the next right and pulled around the corner, so that he wouldn't see her parked there. She parked at the curb. Then, quickly, she scrambled from the truck and walked toward the corner, staying down low behind a hedge, so she could see where he'd gone.

He was just getting out of his truck when she arrived. She saw him slam the door and walk at a brisk pace down the street, his back to her.

Then, checking both ways in a cloak-and-dagger manner, he broke for the houses, slipping through a gap in the fence and dashing between two of the homes.

Very suspicious. And in broad daylight? What was he up to?

Rylie hesitated there for only a moment. Yes, Michael would probably be upset at her. But what if Barney was the killer, and he was going after his next victim?

She took off after him, ducking through the gap in the fence, and quickly followed, crouching down as she moved through the yard.

When she got to the small backyard, she hovered by the bushes between the homes, listening, trying to determine where he'd gone. She heard a door creaking from the house to her right and noticed the back door was open a crack.

Climbing the steps, she reached for her gun.

She could hear him, moving inside, sliding things around and opening drawers. She carefully peered in to a small, bright but old-style kitchen, and noticed the man standing in front of an open drawer, his back to her, emptying silverware into a backpack.

122

A mixture of defeat and indignation swept through her. So Barney wasn't the murderer . . . he was a thief?

She licked her lips, trying to decide what to do. A crime was a crime. She couldn't just let him go. Not after witnessing this. Besides, just because he was a thief didn't mean he wasn't *also* the murderer. He could've been both.

Taking a deep breath, she threw open the door and leveled her gun at him. "FBI! Freeze!"

He stiffened for a split second.

"Hands where I can see them! Move!" she barked.

He started to raise them, ever so slowly, but then, like a bullet shot from a gun, took off for the front of the house.

"Freeze!" she shouted again, but it was no use. He was making his way through the house, for the front door. She let out a groan and took off after him, catching up with him as he scrabbled with the many locks on the front door. Whirling on her, he tried to push her out of the way, shoving her gun to the side as she tried to raise it.

She wrenched her arm away and threw an elbow at him, hitting him in the side of his face as he threw himself for the back door. The force of it knocked him off balance, and he staggered to the side. As he did, she shoved him down, flat, on his stomach.

She grabbed his arm and wrenched it behind him, so that he let out a moan. "Let me go! Let me go!" he whined.

"Not a chance," she said, straddling his middle and bringing her gun in front of his face. "I think you belong in jail for this little stunt. But first, you and I are going to have a little chat."

CHAPTER TWENTY FOUR

Rylie stood at the front door of the strange house, staring at the man on the floor. He was cuffed, leaning against an old sofa, eyeing her with contempt.

No, Barney wasn't exactly like his namesake, the purple dinosaur. He was more like a T-Rex, growling at her, baring his teeth. "I don't know what you want from me," he muttered under his breath. "I ain't done nothin' wrong."

"So you know the people who live in this house?" she asked, leaning against the wall and crossing her arms.

He didn't answer.

"And they're perfectly fine with you relieving them of their silverware?"

Again, no answer.

"Look," she said, sighing. "I'm not interested in whatever it is you're doing here. I called for the local police and they're on their way. I'll have them deal with that. But what I need to know about is what you've been doing while working at the Super Mo-Tel."

His eyes snapped to hers. "What's it matter to you?"

"Because some people have been murdered and it's looking like the killer sourced them from the motel."

His expression changed from aggressive to frightened, almost in the blink of an eye. His eyes widened and he swallowed. "What? Murdered?"

"Yeah. And I'll tell you the truth . . . it's not looking very good for you. I hear you work there as a night clerk, on and off?"

"Yeah, but . . . it's not me." He shook his head fiercely. "I work there when Charlie needs me. That's all. I swear."

"So you don't recall seeing any of these people the past couple of weeks?" she asked, holding out her phone to him, scrolling through the pictures of the victims.

"The past couple weeks? No. Like I said, I don't work there unless Charlie needs me. And he hasn't needed me all month."

Her chest deflated. "You have proof of that?"

"Yeah. Just ask them. They gotta have logs somewhere."

She gritted her teeth. And here, she'd thought she was getting somewhere. She looked around. "And what is all this about? You're a thief."

"Yeah. I take things, now and then. To pay the bills. My parents. They're disabled. I'm the only one who can work and it's barely enough to cover everything."

She nodded, feeling sorry for him. "What would they say if they knew what you were up to?"

His face seemed to crumple. "They wouldn't be happy. But I'm doing it for them. But I ain't no murderer. See, it goes like this. I have a deal with the mailman that works this town. He gives me addresses of places that have held their mail because they're going on vacation, and I let him use the peepholes in the motel, whenever I'm working."

She blinked. "Wait. What peepholes?"

He chuckled. "You don't know about them? Some big, fancy FBI agent you are. There's a secret hall in the back of the motor lodge that goes all the way around the place. You can't see it from the front. But there's a peephole in every room there. The mailman's a bit of a freak."

Rylie winced. Was it true that she'd stayed that night in a place with a peephole? Her stomach squirmed. That made the place even nastier than she'd first thought. "How do you know about this?"

"I'm there at night, and usually, there's nothing going on. So I snooped around a little. Couldn't help it. I found 'em like my fifth night there, out of sheer boredom. They go right into the bathrooms, and some go into the rooms themselves."

Her stomach squirmed. Did people really like spying on other people like that? She never understood the allure. "Do you know how the peepholes got there?"

"No clue." He shrugged, drew his knees up to his chest, and draped his cuffed hands over them. "I guess it's that old woman. Henrietta. Or maybe her son. Maybe they're freaky like that, too. I don't know. I never asked them, never told them I knew about them."

"This mailman . . . what's his name?"

He shrugged.

"You don't know?"

"No. I have no clue. I just met him at a bar a couple times and we got to talking about it."

"And these peepholes . . . do you know if this mailman friend of yours has been accessing them other times, when you're not there?"

"Nah. Probably not. I don't see how he could. Not just anybody can get to them. You can't get to them unless you go through the main office. You have to go behind the front desk, into the back storage room, and there's a secret half-door to the right that they usually keep hidden by boxes. I'd be the only one who'd let him in, unless somehow he snuck in there. Or unless there's another way into that hall I don't know about."

She dragged her hands down her face. Now, she needed to get back to the motel to look for these peepholes and confirm the kid was telling the truth.

He seemed to know exactly what she was thinking, because he laughed. "I wouldn't go asking Henrietta about them peepholes."

She stared at him. "What do you mean?"

"Because she'll deny it and get defensive. She thinks she runs such a respectable place. A family place. Biggest joke. And she might look like a sweet old lady, but she's got fangs. You don't want her on your bad side. Trust me."

All right. Then I'm just going to have to find another way to confirm his story is true. I'll sneak in there, if I have to. No problem.

"Where were you, two nights ago?" she said, referring to the night Bobette Langdon was murdered outside the convenience store.

"Home."

"Alone?"

He shook his head. "With my parents. I told you, they're disabled. They don't go nowhere, and I'm usually there, if I'm not running errands for them or picking up work. I don't got no social life. I've been home. If you don't believe me, go ask them. They're home now. They're always home."

"And last night?"

He smirked. "Home. I was supposed to go to a club in Bozeman with my buddies, but my father wasn't feeling well so I stayed home to take care of him. They're always screwing with my social life. But what can you do?"

Outside, sirens blared. The police, finally here to take Barney off her hands. She opened the door and signaled to them to come in. An officer jogged up the front steps to meet her. "You're Agent Wolf?" he asked.

She nodded and showed him her credentials. "I found this individual breaking into this house and trying to steal silverware," she explained. "He'll tell you all about the mailman he's been working

126

with, who has been giving him inside dirt on these homes that will be empty when residents go on vacation."

He looked horrified. He shook his head. She kicked his shoe.

"Won't you, Barney?"

He nodded sullenly and looked away. "Fine. Whatever."

"But now, if you'll excuse me," she said, heading for the door. "I have another case to attend to."

CHAPTER TWENTY FIVE

Twenty-five minutes later, Rylie stood in the back of the motor lodge, staring at the stark, windowless back wall, cinderblock covered in chipped white paint and mold. It was still day, but back here, against the thick forest, everything was in shadow.

Now that she looked at it, it did seem like there had to be another passage back there. From the inside, the room she'd stayed in hadn't been nearly as big as the building was deep. As she stood on the cracked asphalt, next to an old yellow dumpster, trying to decide what to do, she had an idea.

She walked over to the section of the hotel that had been reduced to a concrete rectangle, due to the fire. It was hidden behind a chain-link fence, and faded signs that said *DANGER: NO TRESPASSING.*

As she moved closer, she noticed that that side of the building was still charred, baring black markings from the distant fire. A clean white, rather flimsy particle-board wall had been constructed there, but even that, now, was covered in mold. She inched closer and noticed, beyond the fence, a slight gap between the new wall and the old cinderblock construction. There was only darkness beyond.

She grabbed her phone and turned on the flashlight, then positioned it strategically so it shone past the fence and into the gap. Sure enough, there was a corridor there.

If the wall was indeed flimsy enough . . .

The fence wasn't exactly the type one would find at a prison. It was only about six feet high, and she was an expert at climbing the fence to get into Hal's property, when she was a kid. Making sure no one was around, she easily scaled it, and hopped onto the concrete pad on the other side.

She went to the wall, and just as she'd hoped, it wasn't well-constructed. She pulled slightly on it, and it came apart, allowing her to slip through the framing. Shoving aside some plastic sheeting, she found herself in a dark hallway. It was so narrow, she had to turn to the side to fit down it.

So chasing after Barney hadn't been a total dead end. He'd been telling the truth, after all. This felt like another piece to the puzzle.

She side-stepped down the dark hall, keeping her flashlight down so that it wouldn't shine into any of the holes. Scraping her hand along the left wall, she found the first one, about two yards down, at chest level.

Feeling like she was doing something she shouldn't, she stooped and fit her eye to the hole. She saw a darkened bathroom, a tile wall, and a shower curtain.

A bathroom.

She blinked away guiltily, even though she hadn't seen anything. It just felt wrong. A complete invasion of privacy. How could people enjoy doing things like this?

Rylie crept forward, feeling for the next hole. Instead, she felt what appeared to be a latch for a sliding door lock. Her fingers moved up and around, feeling a door frame. What the . . . ? There'd been a door into the room, too? She mentally pulled up the layout of the room and realized the door must be in the back of the small closet that had been to the left of the mirror.

So they weren't just peeping, she thought, a shiver going down her spine. *They were going into the rooms. Stealing things, maybe. Or . . . maybe even worse.*

She found another peephole, a few feet away. She didn't look, this time. She found another, and another, her stomach growing sicker and sicker, the farther she went. At the end of the hallway, she bumped into a half-door, just as Barney had said. She found the nearest hole and stooped to look in that one. It looked out into the office. Henny was there, though all Rylie could see was her backside, planted on a stool.

Did she know about these? She had to have. Was she okay with it? Was she involved in it? Questions piled upon questions. The biggest one, though, was . . . was this how the killer spied upon his victims?

Did this have anything to do with the killer at all? Maybe it didn't. Maybe it was just a sick way for someone to get their fun, and was completely unrelated to the murders.

And how long had these peepholes been here? Had they been here for years? Maybe they'd been here for the first murder, almost a decade before. Maybe the prostitute who died there had been spied on that way, too.

Or maybe it all meant nothing. But try as she did, Rylie couldn't seem to shake the feeling that the first murder, all those years ago, had something to do with the new ones. She couldn't explain it . . . but it was the same feeling she'd gotten about this place. A feeling born more of dread than intuition.

As she stood there, she felt more and more uneasy. She needed to get out.

She rushed to the end of the hallway, pushed back the plastic, and squeezed out from the gap in the walls. She climbed the fence and was just throwing her leg over it when a voice from the motel parking lot said, "And what the hell do you think you're doing?"

She twisted unnaturally in her surprise and lost her balance, falling ungracefully to the asphalt outside the fence. She landed on her backside and an elbow. "Ow," she moaned.

It was Michael. He ran around the fence enclosure to the back of the motel and reached down to help her up, but she waved him off and wiped the bits of dirt from her hands and backside.

"Thanks for that. You scared me to death," she grumbled.

"Sorry. I'm noting that you still didn't answer my question, though," he said, peering at the gap in the wall she'd just squeezed through. "Where, exactly, were you, and why did you find the need to trespass?"

He pointed to the sign.

"I've learned a few things since I got here," she said, rubbing her sore elbow. "Can we go somewhere and talk?"

"Sure. I'll buy you a hot dog at Randy's and we can sit in my truck and talk about it. Okay?" He glanced over at his truck. "You didn't mess with it, did you?"

"No," she mumbled. "Of course not. How did I know that our *talking* was going to involve food?"

*

Rylie powered down the window. Though the cabin of his truck was big and luxurious, the smell of chili-cheese from Michael's ridiculously messy late lunch was starting to get to her.

He didn't seem to notice. He licked chili off his fingers and said, "So you seriously hunted down this suspect without me? And you thought that was a good idea?"

She shrugged. "You weren't with me."

"Whose fault was that, again?" He cupped a hand around his ear and leaned into her.

She nudged him off and took a bite of her hot dog, chewing. "Stop. Like I said, if you'd just listened to me when I said that I had a feeling that the crimes were all related to this motel, I think—"

"I'm sorry, I don't go by *feelings*." Orange grease dribbled down his hand. She threw a napkin at him, but he licked at the trail, before it could stain the cuff of his white dress shirt. Gross. "I go by facts."

She scoffed. Was he serious? After what she told him? He couldn't see that it bothered her? Very few things did, but that, he'd simply dismissed. Not wanting to get too personal. Bullshit.

"Maybe, then, when I tried telling you my feelings about my own experience, you should've been a little more responsive?" she snapped.

He stared at her. "What's that supposed to mean?"

"Nothing. Back to the case," she said, avoiding his gaze. "It's a fact now. There's something to do with this motel. Definitely. We just have to figure out what."

He chewed slowly. "And those peepholes?"

"Maybe that plays into it, too. Plus, Beeker told me there was a case of a murdered prostitute, about ten years ago, that happened here. I can't help thinking that might tie into it, too." She finished her plain hot dog and crumpled up the wrapper. "I don't know. That's just a feeling, too. Maybe you're right and the peepholes and dead prostitute are just distractions."

"A dead prostitute?" His lips twisted. "I bet every seedy motel across America has a story of one of those."

"Yeah, but the killer was never found." She looked down at her lap as it hit her. It made total sense why she was focusing on the dead woman. "I guess I'm being silly. Projecting things that have happened to me in the past onto this new case. It probably doesn't have anything to do with these murders at all."

She expected Michael to agree with her, but he shook his head. "No . . . don't be so fast to dismiss it. Yeah, I mean, you went through hell. But just because you experienced that doesn't mean you should dismiss it when it happens again. These patterns . . . they tend to repeat themselves, right? That's what we learned in Quantico. That's why they're called patterns."

Rylie nodded. Then shifted to face him. "You think so?"

He swallowed with some difficulty. "Yeah." She expected him to say some bit of fortune cookie wisdom that he'd gleaned during one of his meals, but instead, he said, "I mean, just look at us. You escaped to Seattle, and I see that look of dread in your eyes every time we cross

131

the Wyoming line. I escaped to Missoula, but you're not ever getting me to go back to Haven."

She blinked. "What?"

He chuckled. "Where I grew up." He wiped his mouth with a napkin. "I'm not ever going back to my hometown in North Dakota. I can't."

"Why?"

A thousand answers to that question swirled in her head, but he simply shook his head. "Maybe I'll tell you some day. Not right now." He motioned to the motel across the street. "Tell me a little more about this secret passage."

Her mind had pulled her away. Was it possible that happy-go-lucky, goofy Michael Brisbane had a dark secret from his past, too? The thought tilted her world on its axis. How would that even be possible? Weren't all people with dark secrets supposed to be tortured, miserable souls . . . like her?

He snapped his fingers in her face, stirring her out of her thoughts. "Hello?"

"Oh," she said, blushing. "Um, yeah. I was worried that Henny wouldn't be happy with us prying into a secret room. Thus my undercover mission."

"There were peepholes to all the rooms? Really?"

"Yep."

"Including the one we stayed in?" He seemed more amused by this than disgusted.

She nodded.

"Hell. Well, then, I guess we need to talk to this Charlie guy and find out a little bit more about these people who stayed here. You think?"

She motioned toward the motel across the street, where a beaten old car had just pulled up. A scruffy-looking man stepped out of it and went to the office, staring at the police car Michael had confiscated. "That might be him," she said. "Henny told me she'd let me know when he showed up."

"All right. Let's go," he said, throwing his truck into reverse.

Rylie tried to psych herself up to interview yet another suspect. But her head was full of thoughts about her partner that she couldn't seem to shake. Did he have a darker and more tortured past than he'd let on? Was this Cheery, Always Smiling Michael Brisbane just a façade?

Who was her partner, really?

132

CHAPTER TWENTY SIX

Rylie and her partner arrived back at the motel just as Henny was stepping out. She saw Henny was wearing her fancy red boots and a cowboy hat.

"Oh, hello, guys and gals," she said with a wink. "I'm going out with my guy, two-stepping."

Rylie frowned. "I thought you were going to call me when Charlie showed up."

"Whoops!" she said, knocking on the side of her temple and hip-bumping Michael. "I forgot! You know how to two-step, handsome?"

He nodded. "Sure do."

Rylie thought he was only joking, being his agreeable self, which may or may not have been only a façade, but then he took her by the hand and they two-stepped around the parking lot. She watched him, surprised at how graceful they both were together. When, giggling, Henny whirled out of his grip, he reached a hand out to Rylie.

"Uh, no," she said, stepping back. "I don't dance."

He motioned her forward. "Come on. You tellin' me, you never two-stepped?" he said, his eyes boring into hers. Some of that slow, midwestern accent crept into his voice, and she didn't like it one bit. "Wyoming girl?"

"Never did. And don't want to start," she said dismissively staring after Henny, who was wandering toward the road. "Um . . . I hope you're not thinking of driving?"

Just as the question left her lips, a boat of an old Cadillac pulled up in front of the woman. Henny lifted her hand and wiggled her fingers, not looking back as an elderly man in a Stetson reached across the seat and opened the door for her. "Don't wait up now," she called, slipping into the car.

They watched it speed off, Michael grinning in amusement.

She looked over at him. "Since when did you become Fred Astaire?"

"There are things about me you don't know," he said with a wink, holding open the door to the office for her.

I know that, she thought, heading inside. *And the funny thing is, I never really cared.*

Until now.

She shook the thoughts away. Obsessing over Michael's past wasn't going to help them find the answers to this case. She found Charlie, standing behind the counter, going through stacks of cash at the cash register. He was almost completely bald on top, but with long dark hair, down to his shoulders, and a long beard that went to his chest, covering up whatever design was on his black t-shirt.

"Hey . . .," he said, eyeing them cautiously. "What are you back here for?"

"So you know we want to ask you some questions, then. Henny was as helpful as she could be but she thought you might be able to fill in the blanks? Considering her eyesight and memory aren't the best?"

He shoved the register drawer closed, making the bell on it ring, and sat down on the stool. "Sure. Shoot."

Michael had already brought the photographs of the victims up on his phone. He shoved it across the counter to Charlie. "You can start by telling us if you recognize any of these people."

He eyed them. "Geesh. These were the victims? Hell," he said, clearly spooked as he brought them closer. "Yeah . . . that one." He pointed to the photograph of Neez. "That one . . ." The photograph of Nick. "He was a real jerk."

"You remember seeing them?" Rylie asked, astonished.

He nodded. "No, never saw that one," he said, pointing to the picture of Bobette. "But I saw this one."

The photograph of Airlia.

"She's dead?" he asked, shaking his head. "Damn. I thought she was pretty hot. I mean, I'm a married man, but I think she was flirting with me."

Michael ignored the comment. "So you checked all of them in, except for her," he said, pointing to the photograph of Bobette. "All right. Can you tell us what you remember about them? Anything stand out to you? Maybe something they said, or did?"

He looked up at the ceiling light, thinking. "Nope, not that I can remember. But hold on . . ." He shuffled a bunch of papers around and whistled. "Woo hoo! Here it is. Yeah, just as I remembered. It's the same."

"What's that?" Rylie asked.

"I gave them all the same room. All three of them. Room six. On the very end."

Michael and Rylie exchanged glances. That felt like it should mean something. She wasn't sure what, but it had to be significant. "On the very end?"

He nodded.

She'd looked into that room from the peephole. The hole had looked in on the bathroom. Something tickled in the back of her head. She had to go check it out. "Is there anyone in there right now?"

He checked the peg board. The key for six was dangling there. "Nope."

"Can I check it out?"

Charlie nodded and handed her the key. "Knock yourself out."

She turned to go there, when Michael said, "Don't you want to finish questioning—"

"You can. I want to check it out."

She bounded to the door and had just opened it when he said, "I thought maybe we could stay togeth—" He stopped and shook his head in disappointment. "Forget it. I'll be there in a minute."

It was only when the door swung shut behind her that she started to feel guilty. She'd already abandoned him once today. And yes, she'd been right about it, but even so . . . she couldn't keep doing that and expect him to follow along like her puppy. He might have played the happy guy who wasn't bothered by anything, but was that really who he was? She'd glimpsed something new about him, before. He was human, and like any human, eventually, he'd get sick of her always expecting to get her own way.

But she couldn't think about that right now. Not with a murder to solve.

Besides, she'd come clean and told him her secret. She'd assumed he'd had none of his own, that he'd had a perfectly rosy childhood, two-stepping his way through life. She hated to admit how much she'd liked watching him dance. He looked good at it, and it had made a hard piece of her heart soften, slightly, in a way it never had before.

And yet, the person he'd showed her . . . was it all a lie? A carefully contrived mask to hide the person he really was? He'd had something so terrible happen to him, he never wanted to go back to North Dakota again. What was that all about? To keep him from his home state, it had to be something big. Or maybe it wasn't. Maybe his life had been so perfect that just being rejected from a college there had turned him against the entire state.

Whatever it was, he hadn't thought enough of her to tell her. She'd spilled her guts to him, told him something she'd never told anyone . . . and he didn't think enough of her to do the same courtesy.

So screw him. You were right, leaving him there, in Wyola. Serves him right.

She groaned as she made her way to the last motel room. *Why do you keep thinking about it? Why do you even care?*

She stopped at the motel room and glanced back to see if he'd followed. No, he hadn't. Good. It was better if she kept her distance from him.

Rylie put the key in the lock and twisted it, then went inside. It smelled musty, like the room they'd stayed in the night before, but the décor was a little different. Instead of rust shag carpet, this carpet was seafoam green. The bedspreads were mauve, and there were paintings on the wall of lonely midwestern landscapes, full of buttes and scrub brush and ponderosa pine.

The door clicked shut behind her, locking on its own. She walked across the room, staring at the two double beds. Three people had spent their last night alive on one of those beds. They'd fallen asleep, with no inkling of the terror they were about to endure. The thought made her knees weaken.

Rylie walked to the mirror, outside the bathroom, hanging on the wall that had the peepholes in it. She looked carefully, running a finger along the mirror's edge, and that's when she found it—a small hole, almost invisible, right beside the mirror.

Unbelievable, she thought, shaking her head as she went into the bathroom.

She knew there was another hole in this room. She'd looked through it, earlier. She found it, cleverly disguised just underneath the towel rack, so small that it looked like nothing but a crack in the tile. She stuck her finger through it, just to be sure.

As she was stooping there, trying to get a better look, she heard the front door open. She assumed it was Michael, so she didn't say anything. He didn't speak either, so she assumed he was angry at her. Again.

Good, she thought to herself. *Let him be. The feeling's mutual. He can two-step his way out of here, for all I care.*

137

He turned on the light, and she heard him, moving around in the room. Who knew what he was doing. Searching for clues? When he didn't come in and see what she was up to right away, she turned toward the door, caught a glimpse in the mirror outside the bathroom, and froze in her tracks.

The man moving through the room wasn't Michael.

It was a rather large man in blue coveralls. He'd placed a bucket full of cleaning supplies on the table. As she watched, he moved around the room, wiping down every surface with a rag.

What was he doing? Wiping away fingerprints? Was he the killer, returning to the scene of the crime?

Don't be silly, Rylie. The crimes didn't happen here. He murdered them elsewhere, remember?

But that didn't explain who this man was. As she watched his reflection in the mirror, he moved closer to the bathroom, until he was almost at the door she was standing in.

Taking a deep breath, she stepped out. "Who are you?"

His eyes widened in surprise. He backed a few steps away, then made a run for it, grabbing his bucket and racing for the door.

The moment he opened it, Michael stood there, his body filling up most of the open space in the frame.

"Michael!" she shouted. "Stop him!"

Michael didn't have to be asked twice. He pulled back and punched him square in the side of the head. The man in coveralls staggered back before falling, unconscious, on the bed nearest the door.

She stared at the man in shock. He was completely motionless, sprawled out on the bedspread. Rylie bent over him, trying to make sure he was still breathing. "Bris, I said stop him, not knock him out, cold."

He massaged his knuckles. "Sorry. But come on. You gotta admit. I *did* stop him."

CHAPTER TWENTY SEVEN

After about fifteen minutes, the man finally started coming to, tossing his head back and forth, his eyelids flickering as his eyes rolled back. Rylie peered over him as they stood in the doorway of the cramped room. There was an angry red bruise on his temple from the punch.

"Hello? Are you okay? Hello?"

His eyes opened, and he looked at her. Then he looked at Michael and winced. He didn't speak.

"Come on, dude," Michael said, helping him to sit up on the end of the bed. "Make it easy on yourself. Tell us what you're doing here."

He eyed them suspiciously and didn't say a word.

Rylie rubbed her eyes tiredly. "This is great. Just what we need."

"Come on, pal. You're not in any trouble. We just want to know why you're here and what you were doing in this room." He pointed to the cleaning supplies. "Why were you cleaning up in here, huh?"

No answer. Rylie shook her head. "I don't have the patience for this."

"You don't say?" Michael said with a smirk, grabbing the guy by the back of the collar. Holding tight to the back of his coveralls, he nudged him forward. "Come on, pal. You're coming with us."

Michael walked him to the office, Rylie following close behind. When they got to the office, Charlie had disappeared. Michael sat him down on the sofa and looked around. "Where's the manager?"

Rylie shrugged. "No idea." She yawned and looked at the man. "Can you tell us anything? What's your name? Where you from? Anything?"

The man just stared.

She scowled at him. Then she said to Michael, "You had your shot at him. I'm about to take mine."

"Easy, easy, easy," he said, coming between them. "Simmer down."

Did he think she was serious? She might have been a loose cannon, but she wasn't that loose. "Okay, mom." She sighed. "What are we supposed to do? If he's not going to talk . . ."

"He can't talk."

They turned to find Charlie, standing in the doorway, holding a soda he must've gotten from the vending machine. He went around the counter and said, "That's Winston Blue. He's local. He was in a bad car accident on the interstate a few years back, and his vocal cords were severed. He's mute. He never learned sign language."

"Oh," Michael said, punching the guy lightly on the shoulder. "Sorry, pal. I didn't mean to . . . well, you know."

"What was he here for, then? He was cleaning the room. I thought Emily was housekeeping and did that."

Charlie nodded. "Winston helps out, too. Emily also waitresses, so what she doesn't get done, he finishes, sometimes. He comes by every few days, when he can." He smiled at Winston. "I'm sure Henny told you this place is a group effort. We all pitch in to keep it going. Even if it's on its last legs."

Rylie shook her head. "Actually, when I first questioned Henny, I got the impression she was the only one who worked here. But people keep coming out of the woodwork. You, Emily, Winston . . . Anyone else I should know about?"

Charlie shrugged. "You probably know she has a lot of people help her out with things. Here and there. Now and then."

Michael sat down across from Winston and began to remove the handcuffs he'd placed on him. He said, "So, you're only here every few days. You see any of the people that stayed in Room Six recently?"

He nodded.

"You were here last night?"

He nodded sheepishly.

"The night before?" Rylie asked, confused.

He nodded again.

Michael stopped working the key to remove the handcuffs and stared at him, looking just as bewildered as Rylie felt. That sounded like a little more than every few days. "Uh, pal, so that begs the question . . ."

"And did you know about the peepholes in the walls, then?" she asked.

He nodded.

Leaving the handcuffs on their suspect, Michael stood up and went to the door. "Hold on. Let me check something." He pointed outside. "That your truck out there? The red Tacoma?"

Winston nodded.

Michael stepped outside. Rylie crossed her arms and looked at the suspect. "So when you came here, the other nights, it wasn't to clean. She only paid you every few days. Were you using the peepholes?"

He looked confused.

"Look. Winston. I know you can hear me. I need to know if you have anyone who can provide you with an alibi for last night, and the night before. Otherwise, you're going to be arrested for murder. Do you understand?"

He looked down, at his lap, still silent.

She dragged in a breath and let it out slowly. The seconds seemed to draw out. She gnawed on the inside of her cheek, then grabbed a pad of paper and a pen from the counter. She slammed it down on the coffee table, in front of him. "If you have something to confess to, you can write it, right? You know how to write?"

He just looked at her blankly, then held up his cuffed hands.

"You're going to write something? I'll take the cuffs off. Let me get the key . . ."

She started for the door, but just then Michael appeared. "I just ran a background on Winston Blue. Seems like our mute friend here has another reason not to talk to us." He looked at the man. "You've got several prior arrests for assault, don't you?"

The man shrugged.

Charlie whistled. "Seriously, man? You know Henny never would've hired you if she knew that. She's all for giving a guy a chance, but come on. Assault? She wouldn't employ anyone who's a danger to her customers."

Michael rolled his eyes in disgust. "Not only that, but I noticed a little something in your car. A gift for us?" He pulled a hunting knife from behind his back.

Rylie's eyes went wide. "The murder weapon?"

"Could be. For at least a couple of them. Want to tell us anything, pal?" Michael said, his voice more of a demanding snarl now.

Rylie crossed her arms and paced the floor, trying to think. Her intuition had been screaming, loud and clear, about this motel. But right now, it was utterly silent. This guy was violent. He had prior arrests. And yet, he didn't seem coldly calculating, like a serial killer. He seemed almost too explosive.

But all the signs were there. And if they made the mistake of letting him go free, and he killed again . . .

She shuddered at the thought. Then she whispered to her partner, "He doesn't have an alibi. He has a weapon, and he has prior arrests. We can't let him go. He's a danger to society. We have enough to arrest him."

"Yeah," Michael said. "My feelings exactly. I'll call the local precinct. We'll bring him in and interrogate him, and maybe we'll get that confession out of him. All right?"

She nodded. "And in the meantime, I can deliver the police car back where it belongs in Wyola. Will you come pick me up later on at the cabins at True North?"

He gazed at her. "Now, why would you do that? Are you feeling guilty for hijacking my truck like that?"

"Maybe," she said. "Will you?"

He found the keys in his pocket and tossed them over to her. "Yeah, I guess. But I meant to tell you, I made reservations for tonight at the Montana Pines. Two rooms, this time. I figured I should, in case they sold out again."

"That's great, because I don't know if I could stand that snoring again," she said, her hand on the door.

He smirked. "You mean, your snoring?"

Had she snored? Maybe. She'd been so tired last night, a bomb could've gone off, and she wouldn't have heard it. Rather than dwell on it, she ignored it. "We might need to stay up there if he doesn't confess right away. I'll see you in a little bit."

She pushed on the door, but suddenly, a thought struck her.

"Hey, Charlie?" she asked, turning toward him. "You know about the murder that happened here, about a decade ago?"

He nodded. "You mean, the prostitute? Sure. I wasn't here for it. But I remember."

"Can you tell me . . . what room did that happen in?"

His brow creased, and for a moment she thought he'd say he didn't know. But then he said, "Room six."

"Oh. And was Winston working here at the time it happened?"

He shook his head. "No. He's just been here the past few months."

She stepped outside and went to the police car. When she was inside, she exhaled, pulled out of the parking lot, and headed east on I-86.

She had a detour to make.

CHAPTER TWENTY EIGHT

Rylie's old neighbor, Hal, had a giant ranch, close to the Montana-Wyoming border. At least 100,000 acres. So many memories flooded her as she took the road leading to his ranch.

Rylie's father and Hal had a bit of a rivalry, for a time. Mr. Wolf had called Hal a crazy old loon and forbid Rylie and Maren from ever playing near his land. Their father had made the man into a monster. But shortly after the death of her mother and disappearance of Maren, Rick Wolf had turned in on himself, drinking a lot, barely getting out of bed most days. In her grief, Rylie had run away. She found herself, miles away from home and hungry, when a storm hit, and she had taken refuge in an old barn.

Hal's old barn.

He'd taken her in, fed her, and talked to her. Turned out, he was a lonely man whose wife had died five years prior. He was a good man, and they'd become friends. He understood when she had her panic attacks, and knew just what to do to keep the demons at bay. He'd encouraged her, when she went off to college in Seattle, during weekly phone calls, and championed her when she decided to apply for the FBI.

Hal Buxton was not just Rylie's mentor and best friend. He was the father she never had.

So it only made sense that she stop by and visit him, now. He'd been wanting her to do so for a month. It was the least she could do.

When she was growing up, he'd lived in a trailer on the ranch, which had an old barn and several outbuildings. He'd since built a log cabin there, something he said he'd been dreaming of since he was a little boy. It wasn't just any cabin, though—it was a rustic estate, with high ceilings, a massive stone fireplace, and windows overlooking his acres and acres of rolling land. The place was a showpiece, even if it was just for him. Rylie didn't know anyone who deserved it more.

As she pulled up the long, winding dirt drive to his home, she was surprised to find herself smiling. She'd only been back here twice since moving to Seattle, and those times had been hard. But now, those feelings of dread that always accompanied her travel to this area of town were overshadowed by anticipation. She couldn't wait to hug Hal again.

Though she'd meant the visit to be a surprise, he was waiting out on the front porch. He'd always been an outdoorsman, though age had slowed him down some. Now, he was nearly eighty-five years old, though he looked twenty years younger, with his full head and beard of snow-white hair. He was slim, wearing jeans, cowboy boots, and a plaid shirt, his normal uniform, and his face was tanned from the sun. He pushed his Stetson back on his forehead as she approached.

"Hi, Hal," she said, standing at the foot of the steps.

"Well, baby girl, this is a nice surprise," he said, smiling. "Come on up here and give me a hug."

She bridged the distance in a split second and wrapped her arms around him. It was just as warm as she'd remembered, but he seemed smaller, more fragile now.

He chuckled and relaxed into her. "You working for the police, now?"

"No, I borrowed the patrol car, and I'm on my way to drop it off," she said with a laugh. He smelled like the smoke from his model trains. "You still working on those trains?"

"Always," he said, motioning to the table nearby, where a locomotive was on its side, atop a bunch of old newspapers. "Weathering that one. You've got to come in and see the layout. I've added a lot since you were last here."

She laughed. Typical Hal. Working with model trains had been his hobby since he was a kid, and he'd never grown out of it. "Of course. You gonna let me run it?"

He laughed. "If you're good," he said, bringing her inside.

The house was gorgeous inside, warm and inviting, with so many windows and that massive fireplace. It'd have been too lonely for most single people, but Hal was a man of many interests. He was hunter, a fisherman, an antique car enthusiast, a history buff . . . he kept himself busy. He took her out past the gourmet kitchen, to another room in the back of the house.

She gasped. The train layout had just been in its infancy the last time she was there, a few unfinished buildings and a proposed track. But now, it was full of cities and neighborhoods and forests and bridges and rolling fields, stretching from one side of the room to the other.

"Wow, you're telling me you've made progress." She beamed at it. "This is incredible."

"Ah, I knew if anyone could appreciate it, it was you."

He sat her down at a stool in front of the controls, and she eased on the lever, just as he'd showed her to, pulling the steam locomotive out of the station. She smiled at the little details he'd added—cars waiting at the crossing, a mother pushing a baby carriage, kids running around a playground. Everywhere she looked, there was an interesting human touch he'd added. He pointed to a girl on a horse, in a field. "This one's you."

She grinned. "You put me in there?" She looked closer. The girl was wearing her hair in braids, just as she always had. She was even wearing the favorite red shirt Rylie had always worn, too. "And where are you?"

"I'm over here," he said, ducking underneath the layout and pointing to a model of a man, standing in the field with a camera, taking pictures of the trains as they went past. He was standing next to a woman in a dress, his late wife.

"Wow," she said, touched, as she eased the locomotive over a trestle bridge. Then she pressed a button, letting the whistle go. "You've captured it all."

"So . . . you in town for long?"

She shook her head. "Not for long. I had a case down this way. It's almost wrapped up, though. I wanted to stop by, before I went back to Rapid City."

He nodded. "You see your dad?"

She winced at the mere thought of Rick Wolf. "Yeah. Don't remind me."

"It didn't go well?"

"No. It did not." She sighed and brought the train to a stop at the next station. It blew out a puff of sweet-scented smoke that she remembered so fondly from her childhood. "He wasn't exactly happy to see me."

"No?"

She shook her head, recalling the moment he'd open the door and gazed at her like some creature from another planet. He was different, too, just as handsome as ever, tall, with his dark hair and piercing blue eyes. There was more salt than pepper in his beard, and his face was bloated and ruddy from heavy drinking. She'd hoped he'd welcome her, but he'd simply said what she'd been fearing all along: *It ain't possible to run away. Ever.*

"He looked at me like he'd seen a ghost. I guess he did, because I look like her," she said quietly. "My mother, I mean. And I don't think he'll ever be able to move past what happened to her."

He nodded. "Well, he wasn't expecting you, was he? You just showed up on his doorstep, out of nowhere, after what? Eight years?"

"Ten," she mumbled. "I would've called, but I didn't have his number. And I wasn't really planning on stopping. It was more of a spur-of-the-moment thing."

"Then I can't say I'd blame him for being a little standoffish, baby girl."

She sighed. That was Hal, a man with a true heart of gold. Rick Wolf had always demonized his neighbor to the north, calling him all sorts of bad things. But Hal hadn't retaliated. In fact, he'd always encouraged her where her father was concerned. Despite all those terrible things her father said about him, he seemed to have more faith in the man than she ever had. "I guess."

"Keep at it. Keep plugging away. Don't give up. Maybe you guys won't ever become close, but you should be open to each other. This life is too short to keep bad blood circulating. Expel it. Right?"

She nodded. He was absolutely right. "Yeah. I'll call next time, before I stop in."

"Good girl."

"The only thing is, he wants to let things lie. To bury it all and ignore it, even as it tears him apart inside. He's always been that way. And me?"

"You?" His eyes flashed to hers.

"I want to find out what happened."

He nodded. "I know you do, baby girl. I would, too. But it's been a long time. And you've been looking that long. Sounds to me like whether you ignore it, or whether you face it head on, you're both in the same place. With that hole inside you growing bigger and bigger. Just don't let it swallow you up."

As usual, he was right. She slipped off the stool, thinking. She wasn't sure what more she could do, where Maren was concerned. Michael had made it pretty clear that he didn't think she had a snowball's chance in hell of finding out what had happened.

He looked around, then clapped his hands. "So . . . dinner? I was going to make barbecue."

146

"I'd love to, but I can't stay long. I have to drop that car off, like I said, and another agent's going to pick me up. At the cabin place at True North. You know it?"

He nodded. "You had a case that brought you that way?"

"Yeah. A serial killing. But we just apprehended the perpetrator. At least, I think." She pulled her phone out and studied it, hoping for a message from Michael, telling her that Winston Blue had confessed. No such luck. "Hopefully."

"Hopefully?"

She sighed. "It's probably nothing. But you see, all the victims came from one motel up near Laurel. I was thinking that this cold case from ten years earlier, another murder of a prostitute at that same motel that was never solved, might have tied into it somehow. But I don't see how it can. And yet . . . "

"Ah. I know how you don't like loose ends."

She smiled sadly. "Right. Exactly. I don't know how to explain it. But I had an instinct that the motel was involved, even when it seemed it wasn't. And it turned out to be right. And I have that same feeling, now, about that other murder. And yet . . ."

"You arrested someone for the murders?"

She nodded. "Yeah . . . but what if . . ."

"What if you arrested the wrong person?"

"Yeah. He hasn't confessed. He had a weapon that might've been the murder weapon. And a record. Plus he doesn't have an alibi. But . . . again . . ."

"Your intuition is telling you something else, is that it, baby girl?"

"Right. It's saying I went off track. I just don't know where."

He pointed to the train set. "Well, you know what happens when one of these beauties goes off track?" he said, picking up one of his Big Boys, a Union Pacific she'd always loved.

"What?"

"You lay on the brakes, pick it up, dust it off, check the track, and put it back on."

She nodded. That made perfect sense. Why did he always say things that not only settled her mind, but make her look at things from a totally different perspective? Obviously, that was what she had to do. Step back, check all the evidence she had for this suspect, and look at it again.

"Thanks," she said, walking to the door. "I think you just helped me."

He smiled and put an arm around her, then kissed her forehead. "That's what I live for."

She jogged down the steps to the police car, gave Hal a wave, and got in. Before she slammed the door, she called, "I promise, I won't stay away long! I'll stop in for a longer visit, soon!"

"You'd better!" he called.

As she took off toward True North, she called in to Michael. He answered right away. "Hey," she said, "What's your ETA?"

"Uh . . . nice to talk to you, too, Wolf."

She rolled her eyes. "I don't have time for niceties. Where are you?"

"What's the problem? I'm finishing up some paperwork for Kit. She wants me to submit it right away. I was going to—"

"You haven't left yet?"

"No. Our guy didn't confess. He's being a total dick, pretending we're not even in the room with him. I don't know. I—"

"All right, well, can you finish up what you're doing and meet me at the Super Mo-Tel Montana? I have a feeling . . ."

"Another feeling?"

"Yeah. It's probably nothing. But I want to check it out."

"All right. Whatever you say," he said. "It might take a while, but I'll get there. Don't do anything stupid in the meantime."

"Of course I won't," she said with a sigh, ending the call and speeding up the ramp onto I-86 West.

CHAPTER TWENTY NINE

The man crouched in his spot, watching through the peephole, as the police came and carted the mute away.

He chuckled as the police pulled him outside, the FBI agent following up. Stupid people. They'd questioned and questioned him, trying to get him to confess when he couldn't say a word. It also meant he couldn't speak in his own defense. So of course, they'd been at an impasse.

But they thought they had their man.

Which meant they'd let their guard down.

So tonight was his night.

He watched through the peephole as Charlie welcomed a woman. She had a fringe of silky straight black hair over her eyes, and a hardcover thriller in the crook of her arm. She was traveling alone. Young and likely foolish. Just what he liked. "It's quiet here, right? I don't want any disturbances," she said, in a snippy little voice. "You can't hear the traffic from the room, can you."

"No, ma'am," Charlie said. "I'm sure you'll be very comfortable."

The woman eyed him doubtfully, then handed over her credit card. The man watched, pressing his eye up against the hole, fingers crossed. When Charlie pulled the key off the peg board for number six, he smiled.

That was just what he wanted to see.

"Here's your card and receipt," Charlie said, leaning over to hand it back to her. "Have a good stay."

"Thanks," she said dismissively, stuffing the items back into her knapsack. She stepped out the door.

Slowly, the man walked down the hallway. He didn't need light. He knew these passages like the back of his hand. They'd been built, many years ago, for moonshiners, during Prohibition. He didn't know the full story, but that's what his mammy had said. Mammy had lived and worked here, devoting almost forty years of her life to this place. She'd known every last thing about this place.

She'd died here, too.

He made his way to the second to last peephole and stooped to peer inside, just as the light to the room went on. This hole was near the mirror, and peered out into Room Six.

As it came into focus, he imagined what he always did, when he looked into Room Six. The sight of his mother, sprawled out on the bed, naked and face-down, covered in blood.

The memory made thick, bitter bile rise in his throat. She'd been stabbed so many times that she didn't even look human anymore. He'd gazed at her, unsure at first what he was seeing. It looked like nothing but a lump of shapeless flesh. But the more he'd stared, the more he'd recognized things, like the gold of her hair, the small birthmark near her temple.

His mother. His beautiful mother. Treated like a piece of meat.

Now, though, he sat silently, watching the woman undress. She paced up and down as she did, first pulling a turtleneck over her head, shaking out her dark hair, exposing a red lace bra. Then, she unbuttoned her jeans, sliding them down over her hips and kicking them off. In her bra and panties, she walked to the mirror and stood right in front of it, so that her midsection was all he could see.

She was a killer.

Oh, she might have been pretty, but then again, that's how they lure innocent people. Innocent people like his mother. She'd made this room her own, her place, because she'd wanted to provide him with the best opportunities available. Henny had allowed it, though she'd never spoken of it. She'd simply say, "Carol, you have a guest," then she'd pocket the money to split, later. His mother would send him into the secret passage.

"Don't peek," she'd say, but of course, the holes hadn't been drilled yet, so he didn't have a way to. And then, an hour later, after the guest had left, she'd collect the money from the front office and the two of them would share hot dogs from the convenience store across the street. Occasionally, his mother would let him get a chili dog, when he was being extra good.

He'd had to drill the holes, though. After that horrible night. Never again would he let anyone pull one over on him.

That night, he'd heard her screaming. He'd wanted to come out and save her, but he'd been too afraid. He was only a boy, then, just twelve years old.

"You need to stay with me, and be quiet, boy," she'd said to him, over and over again. "If you don't, if anyone finds out what I'm doing,

150

they won't understand. They'll send you away. And you'll grow up in an orphanage where they'll treat you terribly. So be a good boy and do as I say."

After she died, though, he didn't have a choice. He'd run away. He'd hitched a ride to Bozeman, worked on a ranch. Told them he was older, and no one checked. No one cared, because he worked hard, and didn't mind it.

He kept looking into it, waiting to see if the killer was ever found. Never was. In fact, the murder was swept under the rug. Sweet little Henny told the police she had no idea who the murdered woman was.

His mother. Carol Baines Seymour.

They knew her as Jane Doe.

And he thought, all the better. Because they also called her horrible things. An unwanted. A prostitute. A friendless nobody.

But he wasn't going to stand for that. He'd had to get his revenge, somehow.

And he would again, tonight.

He watched the woman as she backed away from the mirror. Her hair was in a ponytail now. She reached behind her back, unhooking her bra. She pulled it off to reveal her small breasts, then posed in the mirror. Then she rummaged through her knapsack, pulling out a plain white T-shirt, which she slipped on over her head. She yawned and went for her book.

Sure. She liked to play like a mild-mannered, bookish girl. But that's what they all did. He didn't trust it, one bit.

She was going to have to pay.

Straightening, he stretched, readying himself for the moment. He could see it perfectly. She'd lie on the bed, in the exact place where his mother had breathed her last, and read her book until she grew tired, as if nothing was wrong. Then, she'd turn out the light. That was when he'd strike. He didn't have time to wait for her to go elsewhere. He needed to strike now. He fisted the hunting knife in his hand and licked his lips.

He stooped to get another look, expecting to see her climbing into bed.

But she was still standing there. Staring, almost directly, at him.

She leaned forward, narrowed eyes focused on the hole. "What is . . ." she murmured aloud.

Without warning, she brought a finger up and stuck it through the opening, touching his eyelashes.

151

She sprang back and started to scream.

He placed a hand on the latch, sliding the lock off. He couldn't wait. He could almost hear his mother, calling to him from the grave.

This woman was a killer, and he would make sure that she paid.

CHAPTER THIRTY

The speed limit was eighty on this stretch of I-86, but Rylie pushed a hundred.

The closer she came to the Super Mo-Tel Montana, the more convinced she was that something was utterly wrong.

No wonder Winston Blue hadn't broken down and confessed. No wonder he'd been surprised when she appeared there. No wonder he'd looked at her blankly, uncomprehending her talk about the peepholes. He didn't know they were there. He wasn't the guilty party.

She picked up her phone and called Michael again, hoping that he'd finished up whatever paperwork Kit had him completing, but it went right to voicemail. Cursing, she threw the phone down on the passenger seat of the police cruiser.

Maybe she was wrong. If she was wrong, there was nothing to worry about.

The sign for the Laurel exit came in view. She forced herself to take calm breaths. *No problem,* she told herself. *All you're doing is stopping by the motel to check on everything and make sure all the I's are dotted and T's are crossed. Most likely, you'll find the place just as dead as it usually is.*

And when she crested the top of the hill and saw the blinking VACANCY sign for the Super Mo-Tel, then followed it down to the small structure itself, everything seemed peaceful. Brisbane's truck wasn't there, but there were a couple cars parked in front. Beside the bright light on in the office, two rooms had lights on, too—the one right next to the room that had been destroyed by the partiers, and the one on the very end.

Room Six.

The cursed room. The one that the prostitute had been murdered in, all those years ago. The one that all the victims had stayed in. What was it, about this room?

She pulled up in front of it, watching the window. The curtains were pulled tight, but they swayed a bit, as if someone inside had moved past them.

She stepped out of the police car and noticed the beaten white pick-up truck parked beside her. A sign on the door said, *Seymour the Handyman . . . Service with a Smile!* She'd never seen it before. What was a maintenance truck doing here, at nearly ten o'clock at night? Was it someone just staying in a room for the evening?

She turned her attention back to Room Six. The curtains didn't quite fit the window frame, allowing a small, half-inch gap underneath. She stooped slightly, and saw movement. Whoever was inside certainly wasn't resting.

Just as she lifted her knuckles to rap on the door, she heard the scream. It was coming from inside the room.

She instinctively reached for the doorknob, but it wouldn't twist. It locked upon closing. She knew that from the night she'd spent there. She shoved at it, but it didn't budge. Meanwhile, another scream pierced the air. It sounded like a woman. At that moment, she heard a loud thud and a crash.

Looking around and finding nothing to help her, she rushed to the police car and opened the trunk. There, she grabbed the first tool she found: a pair of bolt-cutters. Wielding it with both hands, she stalked up to the door and brought it down hard, on the knob, again and again. It loosened the first time, but by the third blow, the knob came off and clattered to the ground.

She shoved open the door to find a man she'd never seen before, struggling with a young woman in a white t-shirt. He was on top of her, on the bed, holding a blade up above her, ready to plunge it into her body.

"Help me!" she screamed.

Without hesitation, Rylie lunged forward and swung the bolt cutters at the man's head. The force hit him in the side of the face, but he didn't drop the knife. He simply hopped off the bed and headed in her direction, the knife pointed right at her. Madness glinted in his eyes.

She raised the bolt cutters for protection, and he stopped, just inches from her. "Go away," he snarled, breathing hard.

"Who are you?" she demanded.

He was about her height, maybe a little taller, but his arms were corded with thick muscle. He was fit and attractive, a young man, with deep, mesmerizing blue eyes. He looked nothing like a killer, except for the knife, pointed at her, and the crazy, unfocused look in his gaze. She noticed a patch on his short-sleeve collared shirt that said, *Seymour the Handyman.*

154

"Seymour?" she ventured.

He froze, his eyes narrowing with recognition. The knife trembled in his hand.

Maybe he could be reasoned with.

She spoke in a soft, appeasing voice, "What are you trying to do to that woman?"

He looked over his shoulder at her. She lay on the bed, trembling in terror. "She's a killer. A damn killer. She killed my mother."

His mother.

Of course, the woman who'd been murdered here, all those years ago. The forgotten prostitute. "Who was your mother?" she asked softly.

He didn't answer. He brought the knife closer, ready to lunge at her. She felt the gun at her side, but knew that if she grabbed it, she'd lose the chance to have this end calmly. She couldn't take the chance of angering him further. The look in his eye told her everything she needed to know. He wouldn't go down without a fight.

"Was your mother . . . did she die here?" Rylie suggested.

He sneered at her. "So you know. Were you there? Did you have a hand in it?"

"No . . . it was a long time ago. But I did hear of it."

"Did you? Because you did it? They tried to sweep it under the rug . . ."

"No, I know because I'm trying to solve it. I'm FBI."

He stared at her for a long time. "FBI? You're really FBI? So they do care?"

"Yes, of course we do. We want to help you," she said, speaking as slowly and calmly as she could. "Tell me, what was her name? Your mother?"

He scoffed. "It sure as hell wasn't Jane Doe. Her name was Carol Seymour. And she wasn't a filthy prostitute. She was my mother. And she was killed. Someone came in here and stabbed her to death. I was only twelve when it happened but on that day, I swore I'd come back one day and find whoever did it. And that's what I'm doing," he spat out. "Ridding the world of the murderers, these vile people who don't deserve to breathe air."

Oh, my gosh, Rylie thought, tensing. *He's absolutely insane.*

"Now you know that's against the law. You should leave that up to law enforcement, right?" she said, still speaking calmly.

He nodded, and at first, she thought maybe she was getting through to him. But then his face twisted. "Ten years. You let her rot and you let her murderer get away for ten years. You did nothing!" He fisted the knife tighter, his knuckles turning white as he roared, "You're worthless!"

The woman let out a gasp, and suddenly jumped from the bed and ran for the door. He reached out to grab her, but he only managed to catch a few strands of her ponytail, ripping them from her scalp as she ran, screaming, out the door.

"Bitch! Get back here!" He snarled, taking a step for the door.

But before he could, Rylie slammed it closed.

"I'm sorry. You're going to have to deal with me, now," she said, reaching for the gun at her hip.

They'd gone beyond calmly resolving this. She needed to take serious action.

CHAPTER THIRTY ONE

The second Rylie reached for her gun, the second she had it in her grasp, he was on her. It was as if he knew exactly what she was up to, as if he had his own intuition, guiding him.

The blade came so close that it scraped through the hair near her temple, pushing it from her face. She had to drop the bolt-cutters to grab his wrist and shove the blade away. Her other hand scrabbled for the gun, but her fingertips were slick with sweat, and it fell from the holster to the ground.

He saw it before she did, and went for it. As they dove, they collided, the knife again dangerously close to her. This time, she almost ran right into it. She slipped to the side in the nick of time, but in her clumsy movement she kicked the gun under the bed.

Before she could go for it, he reached for her, grabbing her by her hair. He pulled her mane tight and she felt the hair, popping from her scalp. "Where are you going?" he hissed under his breath. "You come back here."

He pulled her close, back against his hard body, pulling her into a bear hug. She saw the blade, glinting above her in the light.

Before it could come down, she lifted her boot and came down hard, stamping on his foot with every last bit of her weight. He let out a guttural growl, but did not let go. She wiggled, then elbowed back, a move she'd learned in the academy, grabbing hold of his wrist before he could get the knife into position. When she turned, his face was right there. Exposed, in an angry sneer. She bent her fingers into claws and poked at his eye, digging her thumb hard into his eye socket.

He let out a wail of agony, which was enough for her to separate from him, but not enough for her to dive under the bed and retrieve her gun. He screamed, blood spurting from his eye as he flailed the knife in all directions, blocking the door. "Come here!" he shouted blindly, trying to force the other eye to work alone. "I'm gonna kill you!"

She had no escape.

Until she remembered the hidden door in the closet.

Without a second thought, she ran for it. The closet door was open, suggesting he'd sprung from there in order to surprise the woman. It was a small, thin opening, which would probably be a tight squeeze for most fully-grown men. But Rylie easily passed through and into the dark, narrow corridor.

He stormed forth, right on her heels, before she could attempt to close and lock the door.

Her hands fanned out, searching for the way she'd entered before, through that false wall. She knew it was covered in plastic, but all she could feel was the cold cinderblock of the back wall.

Turning, she tried to run, but she didn't know where she was going, and it was absolutely black in there, without even the smallest shaft of light to guide her. She stumbled forward, tripped over something that felt like a small wooden crate, and went down on her knees. A second later, he caught up with her, climbing atop her. Straddling her.

Suddenly, a light filled the room.

Seymour had her pinned, shining a flashlight on her. He leaned over her and looked at her, holding the blade up as if he was about to make a sacrifice and plunge it into her heart. Rylie fastened her eyes shut, but even so, she could feel him silently regarding her. After a moment, he said, "No hard feelings, huh?"

Right. Like she shouldn't have any hard feelings over him killing her.

Her body started to tremble at the thought, betraying every single thing she'd been taught since she entered the academy.

Calm. Just stay calm, she told herself.

But she knew that, just like with any other hardship she'd endured over her lifetime, she was alone in this. Michael was gone, and wouldn't save her. She'd end up dead, just like the rest of them. A sob caught in her throat at that thought, and she did what she'd always done lately when that thought attacked her. She thought of Maren.

She wondered briefly where she was, and if she was even alive. If she was alive, had she ever thought of her, her little sister?

Then she felt the man shifting, moving over her, and she prayed for strength.

Trying to keep her breathing even, she waited for the sensation of the knife digging into her skin, severing her arteries, puncturing her organs. She nearly choked at the thought.

She couldn't let it get that far. If he brought that knife down, she'd rip his arms off.

That's a promise.

At least, that's what she wanted to do. The anger inside her was building, hot and violent, but it probably wouldn't translate to action so neatly. She moved a finger, tried to twitch an elbow at his side, away from him so he couldn't see. Rip his arms off? She probably couldn't have done that with the full use of her body. She'd learned combat at the academy for self-defense, not for aggression.

When she opened her eyes again, they locked with his single good eye. The blood from his wound poured in her face. Face contorting, veins in his temples bulging, he let out an almost animal cry.

And brought he knife down.

She instinctively hurled her body forward, and the knife sailed past her, hitting the cement ground with a tinny *clank*.

"Shit," Seymour growled, taking her by the shoulder and shoving her down. As he forced her back, she saw the panic on his lined face, the fear in his eyes.

Her mind raced. She couldn't get free of him entirely. He was too strong. But the name of the game: Move. Make his task as hard as possible. Scream. And get that knife.

So she did. She screamed as loud as she could.

"Shut up!" he barked, trying to bring the knife back up again. This time, before he could, she grabbed it. She pulled and pried at it with both hands, doing everything she could to get him to release it. And soon, it began to work.

That was it. Her arms clung to him like lead weights, making it impossible for him to get free. She flailed her legs beneath him, jerking him up and down like a bucking bronco, nearly smacking the knife out of his hands. His blood sloshed onto her skin, dampening her shirt.

Seymour hovered over her, caging her in, trying to get her under control as she turned her head back and forth and clamping her mouth closed, making it impossible for him to find a target.

"Sit still like a good girl," he breathed out with exertion, face reddening, the determination in his eye.

He threw nearly his entire weight onto her. As he pressed into her shoulder, nearly overpowering her, only her arm was free to move, her hand frantically feeling around for anything that she could use as a weapon.

Her fingers felt metal, and she managed to drag it forward and grip it. The handle of his knife.

159

Without a second thought, she wrapped her fingers around the hilt and slammed the blade deep into the flesh of his thigh.

His eyes widened in surprise, and he shrieked in pain as pulled back and saw the hilt, buried in his flesh. "You bitch!"

She rolled out of his grasp and scooted her numb body, trying desperately to put space between herself and her assailant.

To her horror, Seymour pulled the knife from his leg without batting an eyelash and advanced on her.

"No!" she screamed. Wobbling to her feet, barely able to stand, she lunged at him, tackling the man by his shoulders and throwing all of her weight onto him. She hit his bicep, the pressure point she knew from martial arts would cause him temporary paralysis.

It didn't topple him, but he did lose control of his hand, dropping the knife with a curse. She clawed him, shoving her fingers into his lymph node, right behind the ear, biting at him like a wild animal, despite her flagging strength.

He shoved her off of him, and she fell to the ground on all fours. Her legs still like jelly, she pulled herself to her knees and tried to make a run for it. She wavered weakly on her knees, as the man began to lunge for her, his hands poised to wrap around her throat.

She backed away instinctively, but he kept coming, until she was pressed against the wall. He kept coming. It was only as he made contact, his hands slipping around her throat, that she heard it.

"Wolf!"

It was Michael.

"He—" she managed to huff out, before he squeezed her windpipe so impossibly tight that she couldn't get any sound out at all.

"Where are you?" he shouted, but of course, she couldn't answer. The most she could do was flail her arms, trying to make some sound to alert him of her whereabouts, but her strength was fading. All sound was drowned out by her own heartbeat. The flashlight he'd shone on her illuminated a small circle of the rafters above her head, but even that was blurring and fading. The man in front of her was nothing but a dark silhouette.

I'm going to die here. With that thought in mind, she fought to push him off her, to rally the strength needed to fight, but it wasn't enough. He kept coming.

"Wolf!" The voice was louder now. Closer.

Brisbane. Had he found her?

160

No. It's too late. It was the last thought she had before everything faded to black.

CHAPTER THIRTY TWO

Brisbane tried to slip through the opening to the secret passage, following the sound of his partner's voice. But maybe Rylie was right. Maybe it was too many big fast-food meals, catching up with him, because he quickly found himself wedged in the gap. He turned to the side, but even that did not allow him the room to step through.

He hovered there, incapacitated, pulse thrumming in his ears as he lifted his Glock and pointed it into absolute darkness.

That was when he heard it. Heavy breathing. A crash. "Who's there? FBI! Freeze!"

He took a deep breath at the door and swung in, his eyes slowly adjusting to the thin light in the enclosed space. There was a man standing at the end of the long, narrow hall, his back to him. He could just barely see another form behind his figure. Rylie?

It looked like he was strangling her, with her weakly clawing at the man. "Let her go!" he shouted.

The man, hunched over her, was so intent on what he was doing that he didn't listen. Springing to action, Brisbane finally wrenched himself through the opening, reaching over and tearing them apart. Then, as he stood there, stunned, the agent drove his elbow into the man's chest. He drove his fist into his face, and the man slowly slumped to the ground.

Crouching over his partner, he inspected her, noticing first the blood caked in her fingernails. Her blood? "Rylie. Listen to me. Rylie?"

Her head lolled like a puppet's and even as she tried to focus, her eyes rolled back in her head.

He lifted her head, stabilizing it, and checked her pulse. It was a slow and steady throb. Floorboards shifted in the doorway and one of the police officers breathed, "Shit, what happened h—"

"Call an ambulance!" he barked at them, touching Rylie's pale cheek. His voice was low. "Hey. Rylie?"

Nothing. He wanted to lift her, move her, but then her eyes closed. He felt for a pulse. It was there, but weak.

"Stay with me," he ordered, his voice hard. "You hear me? Stay with me!"

She gave no indication that she could. He pulled her closer. She'd been hurt before, and badly, but this time it seemed more dire than ever.

He dragged her limp body into his arms. "Stay with me, Rylie. You need to be okay."

Suddenly, she drew in a sharp breath and her eyes flickered.

He sighed with relief. "You all right? Rylie?"

Her eyes focused on him. "Hi," she said, and he smiled.

CHAPTER THIRTY THREE

Bill Matthews sat in his office, staring at the latest national news headline from yesterday, this one out of Nowhere, Montana: *FBI Captures Serial Killer Known For Choosing Victims from Guests of I-86 Motel.*

He didn't need to guess who was responsible for that one. He let out a growl, searching his pockets for a cigarette. He couldn't smoke here, but right now, he really needed one. His face reddened uncomfortably, and a vein bulged in his neck. He pulled at his collar.

What. The. Hell? Even halfway across the country, the woman had a way of vexing him. He'd done everything possible to get rid of her, and yet she haunted him, day and night.

"Rich!" he shouted as he saw the man pass his office door.

"Yep, Boss?" Cooper Rich said, appearing in his doorway. He was holding a cup of coffee.

"Come in. Close the door."

He stepped in and did as he was told. He sat down, concern on his face. "Anything the matter?"

"We need to talk about Rylie Wolf."

His eyes went to the ceiling. Matthews understood. Every time he'd called Rich in, lately, Rylie Wolf was behind it. "Come on, Sir," he said, toying with the lid on his coffee. "She's in the hospital now. From what I've heard, she's doing better, but it was pretty rough, that last case of hers. So give her a break, huh?"

Matthews pressed his lips together. He wouldn't have gone so far as to say he wished that killer would've offed her, but truth be told, it would've made his life a hell of a lot easier. Or maybe not. With his luck, she'd have been elevated to hero status and had a wing of the building named after her. "I understand she's recuperating," he said stiffly. "And I wish her the best. But that doesn't stop the work that I have to do."

He tilted his head. "What work are you talking about? She's not your direct report anymore. What could you possibly have to deal with where she's concerned?"

"That may be so," he said, sifting through the piles of paper, hours and hours of research and digging he'd done. "But as they say, old sins cast long shadows. And I don't want to be caught in the shade, if you know what I mean."

He stopped, mid-sip of his coffee. "I'm sorry. I don't."

"You weren't her partner, but—"

"Rylie Wolf never did do very well with a partner." A smile touched his lips. "I hear she has one, now. I'm sure the guy, whoever he is, must be hating life."

"She went through partners like used tissues because she was too hard-headed and wanted everything done her way."

Rich nodded. "Yeah. But she had a nose for things. When she had a flash of inspiration, she was usually right."

Matthews frowned. So he'd noticed. He hated that about her. "When she had those flashes of inspiration, as you call them, she often went against protocol. I don't have to tell you about the mess she made with that Christopher Thompson case. She destroyed half a million dollars' worth of city property."

"But she found that kid. She saved his life."

Matthews's frown deepened. "Doesn't matter. She gets all the glory for making that save, and yet I'm the one who has to do clean-up and explain to the mayor why the city's budget is exploding."

Rich chuckled sourly. "The explosion of the city's budget has nothing to do with that cushy raise they gave themselves?" He hitched his shoulders. "Look, Rylie's always been that way. Balls to the wall. She does what she has to do to see the results she wants. And the results she wants? Justice served. It's simple as that. That's why she's in the hospital *again,* not for the first time since she headed out east. She doesn't care about herself. She cares about bringing those criminals down."

Matthews peeled a piece of paper off the top of a high pile. "So she's had a few positive results. That doesn't mean that she hasn't stepped on toes. She has, more than she wants to admit. And it's catching up with her."

Rich stared at the paper. "What is this?"

"You don't know? That's what I was trying to tell you. You might not have been her partner, but you must've seen some of the maverick things she's done."

"Yeah, but . . . this is a complaint."

He nodded. "A complaint of unlawful search, made by a man named Moses Bedelbaum. Name ring a bell?"

"Yeah, he was big in the drug and sex slave trade, from what I remember. He's in jail, and Rylie put him there."

"His case is about to come up. But he filed this complaint, which means there's a good chance he can get off."

Rich snorted. "That's bullshit. He's a scumbag and you know he deserves to rot in—"

"Maybe. But laws exist for a reason. If we don't follow the protocol, these people who deserve to be in jail have a loophole. And believe me, they'll exploit it." He paged through the pile. "And I have a dozen more like it, from people who say she treated them unfairly. And it'll be her fault, because she's a loose cannon, if any of these guys walk free."

He leaned forward and sifted through the pile. "I don't . . . where the hell did these all come from? Are you serious?"

He gazed at the younger agent with a solemn face. "It is shocking, isn't it? I'm sad to have to show this to the Deputy Director, but I can't let it go."

It wasn't all that shocking, to him. All he'd had to do was call in a couple favors with the defense attorneys representing these criminals, and with his direction, they'd gone through with the complaints. Now, he had a nice little collection of them. Amazing how the law could be twisted to make anyone look innocent . . . or guilty, as it were. It was all in how you played the game.

And Bill Matthews had chosen a side. Whatever side was opposite Rylie Wolf.

"I don't believe this," Rich finally said, shoving the papers over to him. "You might have something against her, but she's an effective agent with an impeccable record. You can't deny that."

"Her record is flawed." He laced his fingers in front of him. "Deeply flawed. I know you're her friend, but—"

"But what?" His eyes narrowed. "Why did you call me in here, then?"

"I wanted to make you aware. If my father determines there's enough evidence to go forward with an investigation, you may be called in to—"

"I'm not going to—"

"If you withhold information, agent—"

166

"Withhold, nothing! I'm not her partner. I've never seen her do anything against protocol. In my opinion, she's an impeccable agent, and that's all I know."

He waved his hand. "All right. Get out of here. I was just warning you what might be coming up." *And I'm counting on you to tell Wolf. If you do, maybe she'll watch her step and finally start keeping a low profile.*

It was a doubtful. A leopard didn't change its spots. But right now, it was all he had.

He stared at the headline until his eyes burned, then clicked out of it, cursing, and for the first time that morning, tried to get back to work on things that didn't involve Rylie Wolf, the biggest thorn in his side who'd ever existed.

EPILOGUE

"I'm fine," Rylie said robotically from her hospital bed, "But thanks for calling."

She sat up in bed, bored, a soap opera playing in the background. It'd been a non-stop stream of phone calls since she'd been admitted last night, from Kit, then a number of agents from Seattle, then some friends from the academy. She'd been checked over by the medical team for the bump on her head and any damage to her throat and windpipe, and she'd gotten the green light. All she was waiting for, now, was for the doctor to come and sign her discharge papers.

"I'll give you a call!" she said into the phone. "Thanks for checking in."

She hung up the phone and stared at lunch. She'd really been hoping that she wouldn't have to endure it, but here it was—soggy peas, some stuff that was supposed to be chicken in a weird white sauce, and a little carton of milk. She grabbed a Styrofoam dish off the tray, pulled the lid back, and peeked inside. Rice pudding.

Okay.

Grabbing a spoon, she dipped it inside and took a taste. It wasn't terrible.

Her phone rang again. She reached over and grabbed it. As she pulled it to her ear, a voice said, "How's my baby girl?"

She smiled. "Hi, Hal."

"I was just going through the newspaper this morning and whose face did I see among the pages?"

She winced. "Oh, great. Burn that."

"Are you kidding me? I clipped it out. It's hanging on my fridge, now."

She could just imagine that. "Well, thanks, Hal."

"Look . . . I wanted to check in with you and see how you were doing, but I also wanted to let you know. I had an unexpected phone call, this morning. From your dad."

"My . . ." It didn't compute at first. Surely, he meant someone else. Her father had never seen eye to eye with Hal. How did he even have his phone number? "Are you serious? My dad?"

"That's right. Seems he saw the article in the newspaper this morning, too."

Her lips twisted. "And naturally, he couldn't just call the hospital to speak to me himself."

"Well, you know . . .," he let out a short laugh. "Baby steps. He just wanted to know if I'd spoken to you. And if you were okay."

She held the phone, thinking about the last time she'd spoken to him. When she'd checked in on him and said just the same thing. After a decade, she'd stopped by, and he'd been just as confused as she was now. As if every time they interacted, from now on, it would be marked by confusion. But why? Wasn't it natural that they should be concerned? After everything that happened, they were still father and daughter.

"Hmm," she finally said. "Well, if you do talk to him again, you can tell him thank you, and I am okay."

"I told him you always had a way of being."

She smiled. "Or maybe I'll tell him that, the next time I see him."

"All right, honey. You take care. Glad to hear you're on the mend."

"Bye, Hal."

She ended the call and reached for the bowl of rice pudding. As she was scraping some onto the spoon, the music on the television in the corner of the room swelled, and she looked up to see a soap opera couple, lost in their of passion.

"Gross," she mumbled, looking for the remote.

"I don't think I look that bad," a voice said from the door.

She looked up to see Michael, standing in the doorway. He stepped inside, then saw what she was watching on the television.

"Interesting choice," he said.

She finally found the remote and flipped it off. "Believe me, it wasn't my choice."

"Of course not," he said, his tone playful. "You're more of a hardboiled, *CSI, Law and Order* type person, right?"

"I don't usually watch much television."

He moved deeper into the room. "And how are you?"

"Ready to leave. I'm dying here. Can you check with the nurses and see when they might discharge me? I really want to get out on the road."

169

He chuckled. "Whoa. You're pushing it. Don't you think—"

"They already checked me out, and they said I'm fine. I'm just waiting for my discharge papers."

"Well, you'll be happy to know that's why I'm here. They called me and told me you'd be discharged soon, and I figured you'd want to get home as soon as possible."

"Good." He was looking at the tray of disgusting food in front of her, so she pushed it over to him. "Help yourself."

"Really? You don't want an—"

"It's gross. Seriously. Have at it."

He grabbed a fork and started to dig in, scooping a big bite of white chicken and peas into his mouth, chewing slowly. As disgusting as it had looked, he clearly didn't mind it. He motioned to the milk, and when she nodded, he opened the carton and took a swig. Then, more peas. It was as if he hadn't eaten in weeks.

"So did the police release Winston Blue?" she asked.

He nodded, his mouth full of peas, and said, "And yes, Mitt Seymour was arrested for the murders and they've been finding evidence all over his apartment. They were able to identify the body of the cold case a decade back as Carol Seymour, a local woman."

"And once again, you're the big hero. Thanks for coming to the rescue. I wouldn't have gotten out of it without you."

He shrugged humbly. "Well, that's the good thing about partners. So it looks like case closed."

She smiled. "I like hearing those words."

The doctor, a refrigerator-shaped man with a combover, appeared in the doorway, iPad in hand. "Well, Agent Wolf, it looks like you're doing well and your time with us is coming to an end."

She nodded. "I like hearing those words, too."

*

Two days after she returned to Rapid City, Rylie sat in the living room of her crappy apartment in old jogging sweats and slippers, drinking a beer and staring at one of the seventies-style wall panels. Little color blocks from the hardware store had been taped to it. She'd narrowed it down to two, but she still couldn't decide between the pale blue and the pale green.

She hated decorating. Almost as much as she hated sitting around a bleak apartment with nothing to do because her supervisor was making her take a well-needed break.

Normally, she wouldn't have cared about any of this. But she knew that if she had to sit in this terrible, ugly apartment with nothing to do for any longer, she'd probably burst. So she'd turned on HGTV and watched and watched until she felt a little inspired. And then she'd gone out to the Home Depot and bought a few magazines for inspiration. As long as she was going to be out here, she might as well try to make the place look like a home, instead of an old college dorm.

Blue? Or the green? She took another swig of her beer, hoping that being a little drunk would help her make the decision.

As she was about to give up and do eenie-meenie-miney-moe, someone knocked on her door.

"Good," she said aloud. "Maybe I'll have whoever is at the door make the decision. Because this is excruciating."

She opened the door to find Michael standing there, in his typical suit and tie. He'd been the lucky one. He was never sent to the hospital—it was always her, bearing the brunt of the injuries. So he hadn't had to miss any work. He looked a little haggard, with a five o'clock shadow, his tie loosened around his neck.

He was carrying a six pack, and when he saw her beer, he said, "Oh. Well, now you don't have to go out for more."

"You brought me beer?" She was confused. He never stopped by after work.

He nodded. "Yeah. I wanted to . . ." He stopped. "Uh, how was your day?"

"Terrible. I don't care what Kit says," she said, shoving open the door so he could come in and flopping on the couch. "I'm coming in tomorrow. I feel fine."

"All right," he said, hesitating a few steps in. He closed the door and eyed the wall. "You redecorating?"

She nodded. "I needed something to do so I don't go mad. Please. Pick a color. Put me out of my misery. I'm trying to decide between the blue and the green."

He tilted his head. "I like that rust color. That's kind of earthy."

She scowled at him. "I'd eliminated that one. But thanks. I guess I'll add it back in and go a little bit more insane." She eyed him. He was still standing in front of the door, looking around, as if he were

171

afraid of something. "Are you . . .here to gloat about your day at work? Or was there something else?"

"I brought beer." He held it up.

"I saw that. Thanks. Can you put it in the fridge?"

"Sure." He went to the kitchen, opened the refrigerator, and deposited the beer there, returning a second later. Again, he hovered.

She stared at him. "Thanks for bringing it. You can have one, if you want. I mean, you did bring them."

"Oh. Yeah." He went back to the fridge, and returned a moment later, popping the top on the bottle with his keychain bottle opener. "So . . ."

"So?" She stared at him, wondering what he was up to. It looked like he had something to say, but he was afraid to say it. "Is everything all right?"

His mouth moved in a number of different shapes, forming the beginnings of words, as if he was trying to think of the best way to ask her something. But nothing came out.

After about an agonizing ten seconds of this, she said, "Oh, I know. You want to help me paint. Well, thanks, I'll take you up on that." She grinned.

"No—" he started, then swallowed. "I mean, sure. I'll help."

"Good," she said, standing up. "I will buy you dinner first. I'm starving. And knowing you, you're starving too. I have a huge pile of menus from all the restaurants that deliver, left from the last tenant. Or we could just Uber Eats it—"

She grabbed the menus from the drawer and turned around to find him standing, frozen, looking at her. For the first time ever, he didn't look interested in food.

"Okay, what is up with you? I mention dinner and you don't jump all over that like a rabid dog? Are you feeling all right?"

He nodded. "Yeah, but Wolf . . ."

From the look on his face, she could tell it was something serious. She set the menus down and said, "What is it?"

"Well . . . look. It's like this," he said, taking a deep breath. "What I said before about your sister was cruel and said in the heat of the moment. I didn't mean it. And of course, if I can, I want to help you find out what happened to her."

She smiled. "Oh. Well, I appreciate that. But don't worry. I get the feeling you might be right. That it's in the past, too far, and it'll be impossible to uncover anything new. So maybe—"

"But that's the thing," he said, swallowing hard.

She stopped. "What's the thing?"

"I went in to the office today, and I thought I'd look into it on my lunch break. And you know, the new field office has an entire room of cold case files pertaining to this area, from all the other offices, that are sitting there in boxes. There are so many of them, it'll take ages to go through, because they're from years and years past, and they're not in any order. It's like the field offices just threw them together and shipped them off to us, to let us worry about them. Anyway, there was a bunch of stuff that was miscategorized and put in the wrong box, and this afternoon, I found it . . ."

He was babbling now, a mile a minute, and she wasn't quite sure what he was saying. "Do you mean you found something pertaining to my case?"

He nodded and reached into his pocket, pulling out a thin, golden chain. Dangling from it was a small, script M.

A sense of déjà vu flooded her. She hadn't even thought of that necklace, in decades. But the second she saw it, she knew exactly where she'd seen it last.

On Maren's neck, the night before she'd disappeared.

"Where did you get that?" she whispered, unable to take her eyes off it.

He reached for a chair to the dining set and pulled it out for her. "I think you and I had better sit down and talk about this."

NOW AVAILABLE!

WANT YOU
(A Rylie Wolf FBI Suspense Thriller—Book 4)

On a stretch of highway in the Pacific Northwest known for the country's highest number of serial killers, cold cases pile up across state lines, stumping the local police. An elite FBI unit is formed, with brilliant special agent Rylie Wolf at its head—and this time she must crack the case of a string of hitchhikers who've gone missing. Are they all the work of a single killer? And can she save the next one before it's too late?

"Molly Black has written a taut thriller that will keep you on the edge of your seat... I absolutely loved this book and can't wait to read the next book in the series!"
—Reader review for Girl One: Murder

A complex psychological crime thriller full of twists and turns and packed with heart-pounding suspense, the RYLIE WOLF mystery series will make you fall in love with a brilliant new female protagonist and keep you turning pages late into the night. It is a perfect addition for fans of Robert Dugoni, Rachel Caine, Melinda Leigh or Mary Burton.

Books #5 and #6 in the series—TAKE YOU and DARE YOU—are now also available.

"I binge read this book. It hooked me in and didn't stop till the last few pages... I look forward to reading more!"
—Reader review for Found You

"I loved this book! Fast-paced plot, great characters and interesting insights into investigating cold cases. I can't wait to read the next book!"

Molly Black

Bestselling author Molly Black is author of the MAYA GRAY FBI suspense thriller series, comprising nine books (and counting); of the RYLIE WOLF FBI suspense thriller series, comprising six books (and counting); of the TAYLOR SAGE FBI suspense thriller series, comprising three books (and counting); and of the KATIE WINTER FBI suspense thriller series, comprising six books (and counting).

An avid reader and lifelong fan of the mystery and thriller genres, Molly loves to hear from you, so please feel free to visit www.mollyblackauthor.com to learn more and stay in touch.

BOOKS BY MOLLY BLACK

MAYA GRAY MYSTERY SERIES
GIRL ONE: MURDER (Book #1)
GIRL TWO: TAKEN (Book #2)
GIRL THREE: TRAPPED (Book #3)
GIRL FOUR: LURED (Book #4)
GIRL FIVE: BOUND (Book #5)
GIRL SIX: FORSAKEN (Book #6)
GIRL SEVEN: CRAVED (Book #7)
GIRL EIGHT: HUNTED (Book #8)
GIRL NINE: GONE (Book #9)

RYLIE WOLF FBI SUSPENSE THRILLER
FOUND YOU (Book #1)
CAUGHT YOU (Book #2)
SEE YOU (Book #3)
WANT YOU (Book #4)
TAKE YOU (Book #5)
DARE YOU (Book #6)

TAYLOR SAGE FBI SUSPENSE THRILLER
DON'T LOOK (Book #1)
DON'T BREATHE (Book #2)
DON'T RUN (Book #3)

KATIE WINTER FBI SUSPENSE THRILLER
SAVE ME (Book #1)
REACH ME (Book #2)
HIDE ME (Book #3)
BELIEVE ME (Book #4)
HELP ME (Book #5)
FORGET ME (Book #6)

9 781094 394695